MW01681126

John Miles

The President's Bodyguard

The President's Bodyguard

By John Miles

Four Seasons Publishers
Titusville, FL

The President's Bodyguard

This is a work of fiction.
All characters and events portrayed in this book are fictional, and any resemblance to real people is purely coincidental.

For information contact: Four Seasons Publishers
P.O.Box 51, Titusville, FL 32781

PRINTING HISTORY
First Printing 2001

ISBN 1-891929-59-3

PRINTED IN THE UNITED STATES OF AMERICA
1 2 3 4 5 6 7 8 9 10

A special thanks to Lynn Pike for her diligent efforts in the preparation of this novel.

The time is shortly after the turn of the twenty-first century. The nation is divided over a presidential election and the world seems to be rushing toward a climax. The division is not so much centered in political parties but in religious matters. One group is called the Creationist Group. The other is called the Humanist Group.

The condition of America has deteriorated in every category, and the spirit of anarchy is in the air. The life of America is hanging by a slender cord. What will be the outcome?

Chapter One
Heritage

Todd Bradley was deep in thought as he turned into the country road that led to his family home. Four months away seemed like a year with all that had transpired. Washington, D.C. was like a foreign country compared to rural Spring County and the town of Cloverdale.

This was home, where he had lived somewhat as an athletic celebrity, reaching all over the state as a high school and college champion wrestler. He relived those days in his thoughts as his eyes took in the familiar landscape of houses and farms and woods and animals.

What a change from the nation's capital where he had lived the last four months in training for Special Security Forces, particularly for guarding high government officials. He had been nominated for that elite body of men by his congressman who had taken a special interest in his athletic success and high academic record both in high school and college.

He and the other men were strictly on trial as they were put through physical and mental disciplines designed to bring to the top the cream of this crop. Several were washed out during the training, but Todd was among those who were selected for Security Corp. Those selected were sworn in to government service at an impressive function attended by the new President himself. They were granted a two-week leave to go back to their homes. They were told that they would be called at their homes and informed of their assignments. Todd was filled with suspense as to what his would be.

His reverie was interrupted when he came to the property line of his father's farm. The farm included about a thousand acres of rich farmland, pasture and woods which merged into a state forest that was several miles deep.

Todd was surprised to see the beginning of a six-foot woven wire fence that now evidently encompassed the entire farm. He drove along it now until he came to a strong gate that barred the entrance to his family home.

His 12 year old brother, Tom, was there to open the gate. With him were two huge German Shepherd dogs challenging the new arrival with deep throated barking.

Todd drove through the open gate and then stopped to let Tom into the car so he could ride up to the house which was set back some distance from the road. Todd hugged his young brother as he got in.

"How long have you had the fence and the gate?" Todd asked

"About a month," his brother replied. "We had to install it to keep from being robbed."

The dogs were running ahead of the car announcing their coming.

"I hope the dogs still know me," Todd said. "They were my close friends for two years, but they may have short memories. They sure look bigger than when I last saw them."

"I'm sure they will know you. We'll soon find out," Tom laughed.

As they came down the lane, Todd drank in the beauty of the large, old farmhouse and the adjoining buildings. There was a large barn looming behind the house and hiding the corral. There were sheds, corn cribs and silos on one side and an assortment of tractors and farm machinery on the other.

There was an air of expectancy in the house. Todd had called from the airport in Kingston to tell them about when they could expect him. Sue, his mother, and Tess, his 15 year old sister, had the table set and food ready for supper.

Bill Bradley, the father, and his 17 year old son, Tim, were in the living room resting from barn chores and watching for Todd to arrive.

"Here he comes," Tim announced, and there was a rush for the back door.

Todd drove his car to the back of the house and got out. The first greeting he got was from the dogs. They recognized him and were all over him. Todd hugged and kissed his mother and Tess. Then he turned and shook hands and hugged his father and younger brother Tim. The boys grabbed his suitcase, and they all headed in to the kitchen.

"As soon as you freshen up a bit, we will eat supper", Sue said.

"I can hardly wait," replied Todd. "Oh, how I have missed your cooking." With this, he started toward his old room carrying his suitcase.

"Don't go there," his mother warned. "Tim has taken over your room. You sleep in the guest room while you are here."

"Well, how do you like that," Todd quipped. "I leave for four months, and someone steals my room," he said with a laugh.

He looked around the guest room and thought about how many people had enjoyed the hospitality of his parents. He then thought of the warmth of this home and the love of one another in his family. He wondered how he would do in Washington. He thought about the fact that now it was the turn of the 21st century and how sharply divided the nation was over the presidential election, and how he sensed that Washington was a boiling caldron politically, and one had the feeling that anything could happen. All the new men in Special Security Forces sensed that they might be in the center of an explosive situation.

In their talks with one another, some questioned the wisdom of making the Security Forces their career. The thought flashed across his mind, "Why should I leave the peace and security of this home and community for the danger and unrest of the nation's capital?" He wondered, "What will be my assignment? Will I like it?"

He quickly threw off these thoughts and made his way to the dining room. The family was all there, standing, waiting for him. They all sat down and the father gave thanks to God for his son's safe trip and for the food. Supper was a joyous time as they talked about some of the things they had done as a family in the past. Gradually, the ladies cleared the table as each course was consumed and they had finished off the dessert. There was an air of suspense because each person had questions to ask Todd but did not feel easy about asking until the table had been cleared.

Tom was young and impatient. He was itching to ask the first question. Todd was his hero. The walls in his room were covered with newspaper clippings and pictures of Todd's exploits on the wrestling mat. He was especially proud of the awards Todd won at State College when he was champion for two years in his weight class, in the league which covered several states. He wrestled at 198 pounds, and Tom longed to increase his 115 pounds to the weight of his brother.

"Todd, are you going to be a bodyguard," he finally burst out.

Todd smiled fondly at his brother. "I think I will be a bodyguard of some kind, but we haven't been told our exact assignment yet. They promised to call us at our homes within this two-week period and tell us. I wish I could tell you more, but that's all I know. I'm sure you will all have your answer before I go back to Washington."

"Before we get to anything more about me," and here he turned to his father, "How are things going around here? They were heating up a little when I left, and I noticed the new fence and the gate as I drove up today."

"Let me give it to you straight," Bill replied. "It was bad enough when you left, but it is much worse now."

"You ought to visit the school now," Tess chimed in. "Tom and I are being home-schooled."

Mr. Bradley continued, "That's true. Things just got so dangerous, and the classroom setting so difficult for learning and teaching that we pulled Tess and Tom out. Tim still goes to high school because he is nearing graduation and is so involved in sports. He drives the pickup to school because the school bus is a nightmare."

"I had no idea it had gotten that bad," Todd broke in. "Washington, D.C.—yes, other cities—I can understand, but Cloverdale—It doesn't seem possible."

"I'll tell you just how bad it is," his father said sadly. "Your friend, superintendent Baxter, is still in the hospital. He was attacked in the restroom of the school by four young toughs, and they almost killed him. He had expelled one of their buddies for fighting and stealing. All four of the assailants are in jail, but there are plenty more just like them still in school. On top of all this, the parents of the five boys have called in the organization "LFCR" (League for Citizen's Rights) to sue the school board and the superintendent, claiming class discrimination in the school and particularly against these boys. That will be facing Mr. Baxter when he gets out of the hospital. There isn't a shred of evidence in this all-white school. But they don't need any evidence to win their cases anymore."

Todd stared at him, aghast at what he had just heard about his school.

Tim broke in, "Most of the athletes are fairly good kids. They are the ones I hang around with at school. The rest of the decent kids do likewise. We never go into the restrooms alone, that is just inviting trouble. We go there with three or four at a minimum. That is the class situation they will try to prove in the courts. In reality, it is the rebels, drugs and alcohol users, cheaters, and disturbers in classes on one side, and the decent students who want an education on the other side. It is a class distinction by the student's choice."

Todd rejoiced inwardly at his brother's insight and analysis. He thought back at the tremendously good heritage he and his brothers and sister had been favored to have. This was a Christian home, and their father and mother were wonderfully wise and consistent in their lives and instruction.

Todd shook his head, "How could it possibly have happened so quickly?"

"It didn't happen quickly, son," Bill responded. "It existed to a certain extent when you were in high school and then blossomed out while you were in college. It exploded this last fall. But everything has seeds and roots. This may seem like over simplification," the father asserted as he drew closer to the table, "but it goes back to two Supreme Court decisions: One - the decision that gave power to take God and the Bible out of the schools, taking away all authority for judging what is right and wrong; and Two - the decision of 'Roe vs. Wade' that made legal the killing of babies in the womb, which has eroded the value of human life. Our country has chosen to be godless, and we have reaped and are reaping the fruits of it."

Todd exclaimed, "I expected this in Kingston, where I flew in, because it is a large city; but I didn't dream it could happen in our small town of Cloverdale, just six miles from our house."

"We take the Kingston paper," Bill continued, "Riots, killings, and looting are daily and nightly events, just like Washinton, D.C."

"And now, our town of Cloverdale, where you went to high school, which used to be such a peaceful and trusting community, is wracked by the same kind of crime and violence that is in Kingston. Some banks are closed, people are out of work, and stores have turned into armed forts where the owners sleep at night with loaded guns to protect their property. All this is reaching out into the rural areas. Many farms have been raided, and we all have to take precautions."

"This may seem strange, but one of us, either Tim or myself, has to stay home from church on Sundays or our place would be raided. We keep the gate to the lane closed and locked day and night. The two German Shepherds, that were raised by you, roam the premises. The big hound, Bell, that we all hunted with, lives in the fenced-in area where the livestock are kept at night. If anything unusual comes near there, he sounds off with a howl that can be heard a half mile."

"Some farmers have been cleaned out in one day or night. A whole group of farmers met with the Sheriff's Department and the State Police. They told us it is little use to call them. They will do their best to come, but they can't possibly keep up with the calls. They told us to defend our own property with fences, dogs and guns and not to count on them too much."

Todd was not surprised at this account, but he was saddened that the degeneration of the nation had affected his own family, making them virtually prisoners in their own home. He was grateful they were on a farm.

Quiet settled over the family, and Todd sat, full of his own thoughts. He loved his parents dearly, and he sensed the burden they bore. They had led each of their children to the Lord, taught them the Bible, taken them to a Bible-teaching church, and lived as proper examples of what a Christian should be.

Mr. Bradley was an all-around man. He had taught his children how to work. But he also loved to hunt wild game, and his wife and children all joined him in that interest. He taught them how to handle and use firearms and how to stalk, track, and shoot. Their wooded land backed up to a state forest where hunting was permitted.

Todd wondered if his father and family would use their guns, of which they had many, to defend themselves. The whole countryside knew the reputation of this family and their guns and hunting skills. Perhaps that knowledge and reputation alone, being widespread, would keep thieves away and the family would never have to use their guns. Todd prayed that it would be so.

Sue, Todd's mother, broke the silence and brought Todd back to reality.

"What do you think of all this?" she asked.

"I am flabbergasted," he answered, "But I was just lost in thought over what is going on here. You folks may be concerned about me in Washington, but I sure will be concerned about you out here."

Todd highly respected his parents. They were very well read, students of history, deeply involved in the church, and active in trying to get good people into office.

"Dad, I respect your opinion on the whole national situation. I know we were all terribly disappointed in the last election. We thought we might at least have had some reason for hope for our nation if our Creationist man had won the presidency. But it didn't happen. How do you read things now?"

"Well, I must admit that I was terribly disappointed when Jackson was elected, and it is still a discouraging situation," Bill answered gravely. "We ended up with three parties and three presidential candidates, and that did it. All the off-beat groups got behind Jackson, and his campaign was engineered by some real pros' who are unsavory, questionable characters. Jackson didn't declare himself on any moral issues. He didn't have to. I'm afraid we are in for big trouble, and our country cannot stand for any more. We may be going down the tubes."

"That analyzes it very well, Dad. All of us had high hopes of changing the Supreme Court, but those hopes have been pretty well dashed. Jackson isn't likely to nominate a pro-life man to the Supreme Court."

"I have met the President just one time. That was when we were sworn in. He seems like a nice fellow, and his wife is a delightful lady, very natural and genuine. I had a chance at the reception to talk quite a while with her and her personal secretary. Her secretary is beautiful and impressed me greatly. For some reason they seemed to seek me out and asked me a lot of questions about myself. Probably they did the same with the other men as well."

The conversation then changed to other questions about his

training and Washington.

Finally, Bill announced it was time for him to make his nightly rounds before he went to bed. Todd and the boys said they would go with him. All was quiet as they walked around the buildings and checked the cattle and the horses in the barn and the corral. Bell greeted them with a howl assuring them that he was on duty. They then made their way back to the house.

The next two days Todd helped his father with the farm work and mixed in long talks with his mother in the kitchen.

The third evening they were eating supper when the phone rang. Tess answered, and a voice announced it was Carl Bangor, head of Security Forces in Washington, calling for Todd Bradley. Todd took the receiver, and the family watched and listened intently.

"Yes, this is Todd—I'm doing fine, having a great time at home—What is it?—Are you sure?—I didn't know such a position existed.—Where will I live?—No kidding?—I'll be looking forward to seeing you when I get back to Washington.—Thanks for calling—Goodbye."

Todd came back to the table and sat down.

"Well," Tom said, "What did he say?"

"He asked me how I was doing here at home, and I told him I was having a good time," Tom replied.

Tess spoke up impatiently, "Stop teasing us, Todd. What is your assignment?"

"I have been assigned to be the personal bodyguard of President Jackson, and I am to live in my own apartment in the White House. Can you believe that?"

The family was stunned. "Are you sure about this?" Tim asked.

"It was the head of security who called me, and he should know if anyone does. I'm sure."

Mrs. Bradley turned her head and tried to hide her tears in her napkin. What she saw was the great danger to her son as he would be protecting the President.

The children all beamed. They saw the glamour and glory of

such an assignment.

Across the father's mind flashed the danger, and yet the importance, privilege and honor of this opportunity. He saw God working in his son's life.

Tess was a thoughtful girl and spoke what was on most of their minds as the announcement sank in, "Maybe God is going to use you, Todd, to bring some changes in President Jackson."

Thank you, Tess. Who would ever anticipate that I would be moving right into the middle of it all, keeping company with the President. It is awesome. Maybe I can be a Daniel or a Nehemiah in my new position."

Bill was very thoughtful as he spoke, "Son, I want you to know that I am very proud of you from a spiritual standpoint. We dedicated you to the Lord from birth to do God's will. We did the same with the rest of the children.

"It would be nice and comforting to have you here working on the farm with me, but I can see that God has other plans for you. I know that God will care for you in this new position, and no harm can come unless God wills it. You are equipped with a great knowledge of the Scriptures, God has given you an excellent body and mind, and He alone knows how He may use you in influencing the President for God."

His mother left her chair and came around the table towards her son. Todd arose to meet her, and they embraced—she looked up into his face with tears running down her cheeks and a radiant look on her face that touched his heart, and his tears started to flow.

"Son," she said, "When you told us what you would be doing, tears of fear began to flow, because I love you so; but then I remembered what God said, 'Do not be anxious about anything' and peace came over my heart. Then I remembered how we had dedicated you to God and to His will, and now I am shedding tears of joy for how God is going to use you. You go with our prayers and our blessing." Then she began to sing softly, and the family gradually joined in: "Be not dismayed what'er betide. God will take care of you."

Todd spent the next few days looking up his friends, helping his father, watching his young brother Tim at a wrestling meet, attending their small church, and spending hours talking with his family.

Time went swiftly, and he found himself on the plane flying back to Washington. Arriving there, Chief Bangor called a meeting of all the men, called their names and announced their assignments. A murmur went through the group when Todd's assignment was announced.

When the meeting broke up, several of the men congratulated Todd, others joked and said, "Where did you get your pull? Who do you know in Washington?"

Chief Bangor called Todd to the front and told him he would take him to the White House to get located. Arriving there, Todd was shown a small, well-furnished apartment, complete with kitchen facilities. He was told that someone would see him later and acquaint him with the procedures of the White House. Bangor left him saying, "Continue your training program with the other security men until you receive directions from the White House."

Chapter 2
Confrontation

Bo Campbell entered the locker room of the Special Forces gymnasium. He entered the left aisle and stopped at his locker. As he began to undress, he pondered his own dark mood. The last time he had been here for boxing he had had a run in with the trainer, Rusty McGiddo. If that wasn't bad enough, his sparring partner scheduled for today was Todd Bradley, a man he disliked very much. On the other hand, this match he might enjoy! Perhaps he could take some wrath out on Todd because he was a wrestler, not a boxer.

Bo had his boxing trunks on before Todd entered the locker room. Todd's locker was in the other aisle. They knew one another's presence by the rattling of the lockers. "Hi, Bo," Todd said, as he started to change clothes.

"Hi," Bo grunted, heading for the scales to avoid further conversation. The scales were at the end of the aisle where Todd was getting into his boxing trunks. Behind the scales was a full-length mirror. Todd watched as Bo weighed in. He was six feet tall and weighed 250 pounds. Bo had been a line backer in college, a little slow, but had an uncanny ability to sense plays, and he was noted for his hard hitting and sure tackles.

Bo gave himself the once over as he glanced at the mirror: black, unruly hair; rather handsome, wide face; piercing, dark eyes; muscular arms and shoulders; a barrel-chested body going almost straight down to his hips, and sturdy legs. His teammates called him "Bull" in college because of his rugged appearance and fierce playing. The features that drew one's attention the most were his eyes and mouth. The eyes were penetrating and challenging. The mouth was turned down at the corners just enough to give a cynical, and at times, sinister look, which Bo sought to disguise. Bo completed the chart which Rusty, the trainer required; laced his boxing shoes; and made his way up the stairs to the gymnasium, carrying his head gear in his hand.

Todd Bradley was apprehensive today, not because he was afraid of Bo, but because he disliked confrontation and the rising barrier that existed between the two men. He pulled on his boxing shorts and walked to the scales. His weight read 198 pounds. He, too, looked in the mirror and grimaced over the thoughts he was having. Anyone else seeing the reflection in the mirror would have seen a man 6'4", 24-years old, blonde with blue eyes, a handsome and kindly face, firm with a ready smile. His body was well proportioned with broad shoulders and narrow hips, muscular and quick in his movements.

As he completed his preparations for boxing, his mind went over the events of the past few months. He had seen both hate and jealousy in Bo's eyes and reactions. They had entered the government's Special Forces Program at the same time. They had the same training, and they both had their assignments. From the beginning of the program, which was very demanding, they moved toward the goal of becoming proficient in the use of firearms, boxing, wrestling and the martial arts.

Today, a boxing session was scheduled between Bo and Todd. The trainer was Rusty McGiddo, once a professional boxer, then a manager, now a trainer of government bodyguards. He was tough and a stickler for rules, but he was fair and occasionally showed a kind side as well.

Todd had readily taken to boxing and martial arts. He was a natural athlete and liked the challenge of any new sport. Rusty spent extra time with him in boxing and longed to see him try the professional ring, but Todd had no interest in that at all.

Rusty and Bo were waiting for him, as he entered the gymnasium and made his way to the boxing ring. Todd held out his hands for Rusty to tie on the gloves. They were big gloves, well padded, designed not for damage to the opponent but for developing finesse in boxing. As Rusty tied on the gloves, he instructed both men concerning the rules as to when and where not to hit, foot work, and various aspects of boxing.

They took their respective corners and came out cautiously with the bell. Todd watched Bo's eyes, where he saw hatred and determination—probably to do damage. Todd's primary purpose was to put into practice the principles that McGiddo had drilled into him. He had the reach on Bo, and his left hand was constantly in the shorter man's face. Bo was frustrated with this and sought to bore in by sheer strength and weight. But Todd's footwork was superb, and he was quick as a cat. Bo resorted to rushes and wild swings and was wide open for Todd's right punch every time he lunged. Todd refrained from taking advantage of the heavier man lest he humiliate him.

Suddenly, Rusty blew his whistle and stepped in. "Bo, you are not boxing. You are flat footed, and you are not doing anything that I have tried to teach you. And, Todd, you are not taking advantage of the openings that come your way. Bo will not learn defense unless you nail him when you can. Now, let's get some sense into your heads and practice the things you've learned."

They started boxing again, and for about fifteen seconds Bo tried to maintain a boxing stance and to be light on his feet. But he had been brought up on street fighting and he still thought he could whip most anyone by overpowering them. Todd's left burned his nose, and he threw all caution to the wind. With a bull-like charge, he came in flailing the air. Todd did not give ground, but hit Bo squarely on the jaw, and even with the big, cushioned glove, knocked him down.

Bo, humiliated and angry, pulled himself to his feet. He charged Todd again, and this time his objective was to break through and butt Todd's jaw with his head. Todd sidestepped the rush, an at the same time smashed another right to the side of Bo's jaw that sent him reeling into the ropes and then flat on the floor.

That was enough for Rusty. He blew his whistle. "Okay, that's enough for today. Bo, you haven't learned a thing since you boxed Smitty. You still think you're playing football. That doesn't work in boxing. Go take a shower."

Bo glared as Rusty untied his gloves and then headed for the locker room. Todd untied his gloves with his teeth. "Come into my office," Rusty said to Todd. When they were settled in the office and drinking some pop, Rusty said, "What's with you two? It's obvious that he hates you for some reason and would like to knock your block off if he could."

Todd thought a moment. "I really did not want to humiliate him. That's why I didn't take advantage of openings during the first part of our match."

"I figured that," said Rusty, "but I knew Bo would never learn unless he was taught the hard way. Tell me, why does he hate you?"

"I can only think of two reasons," Todd began. "One is something that happened in our first session with Jud Wilcox, the wrestling coach and trainer. In the midst of Jud's preliminary instructions about the value of knowing how to wrestle and render an opponent helpless without hurting him, Bo spoke up, 'Wrestling is kid's stuff. I bet I could whip any of these guys in wrestling, and I've never had lessons.

"Jud had a profile and history of every man in his wrestling class. Just like you have, Rusty, in boxing class. Well, Jud said, 'Okay, tell you what I'll do. I'll pick one of these fellows who is about your size and let you wrestle, and we'll see how it goes.'

Todd went on, "Jud looked over the men and said, 'You,' pointing at me, 'What's your name?'"

"I said, 'Todd Bradley.'"

"Jud said, 'How much do you weigh?'"

"I said, 'About 200 pounds.'"

"'Have you had any wrestling experience?'"

"I answered, 'Yes.'"

"Then he turned to Bo and said, 'What's your weight?'"

"'Two-fifty,' replied the confident Bo with a smirk, 'You better get someone with a little more beef.'"

"'Bradley, are you willing?' Jud asked soberly."

"'I'm willing to give it a try,' I said."

"Jud got us both out to the middle of the wrestling mat with all of the security class looking on. He said, 'When I blow the whistle, start.' He blew the whistle and I went for Bo's legs. About five seconds later, I pinned him. Bo struggled and grunted for several seconds until I let him up. Bo was thoroughly humiliated when the other men laughed. I knew by the look that Bo gave me that I had made an enemy."

Rusty took a deep breath. "Wow. I'm surprised Jud never told me about that. I understand now. What's the second reason he hates you?"

"Well, I don't know about his feelings about this for sure, but perhaps he is jealous over my assignment as the President's personal bodyguard. All the other guys have been kidding me about the pull that I must have had to get that job. I notice that Bo just clams up and looks dark when the fellows talk about it. It's hard for me also to figure out how I got that assignment, but I like it and take it seriously."

"Well, if I needed a bodyguard," Rusty said with a shake of the head, "I can't think of anyone I would rather have than you. You have all the skills, and you're quicker than any fighter I have ever fought or worked."

"I was talking with Jimmy Rin, the martial arts instructor, the other day about you. He said you have caught on quicker than any student he has ever had, and that you already are as good as he is. Now that's some compliment."

"Thanks for telling me, and thanks for your confidence, Rusty. I hope I can live up to all of that. From the first time I met you, I felt that we could identify with each other."

"Thanks, Todd," the older man said. "I sense we have a lot in common. We may be able to help each other."

Todd made his way out the door and back to the locker room. Bo had already showered, dressed, and was gone. Todd had a strange feeling that there was more behind the animosity of Bo than the incidents that had occurred. Little did Todd know just how much this man would have to do with Todd's future.

Chapter 3
The President

Todd made his way back to the White House. The whole thing was so bizarre that it went beyond his understanding. He was not used to having enemies. Good natured himself, having many friends wherever he was, he had never had the experience of looking into another's eyes and seeing such vicious hatred as he had seen in the eyes of Bo.

Then, on the other, hand, what could be more bizarre than he, a country boy, living in the White House and being the President's personal bodyguard? The President had been inaugurated only a few weeks ago, and not long after, Todd was living in his own apartment in the White House.

The whole Presidential family and staff were still feeling their way in their new quarters. Todd had received no special instructions except that he was to be available to the President at any time. He had been informed earlier in the day that the President would contact him that evening.

As he entered his small apartment, he went over the things he had learned about the people he had met among the staff. He had the option of eating his meals with the food service staff or fixing meals in his apartment. Most of the food service personnel were veteran employees, but a few new employees had been forced upon them by the victorious election party boss, Mike Burly.

Todd had gotten acquainted with the head of food services, June, a lady in her forties. She was a loquacious lady when you got on the right subject and if she trusted you. She was a clear thinker and had an uncanny ability to analyze people. She had a great sense of humor that drew people to her; however, she did not cultivate the friendship of anyone that she thought was a fake in any way. She was courageous enough to tell the President himself the truth about himself if he asked her. She had never married, but seemed to consider her single life an advantage rather than a disadvantage. She was a very skilled food service director and a hard worker as well. Often, she would prepare a meal by herself when schedules called for it.

Todd had walked into food service one day just after a meal, when she was eating by herself. He introduced himself and discovered that she was head of food service.

"Have you had supper?" she asked.

"No," he answered, "but I plan to go to my apartment and fix something."

"No use doing that. We had plenty left over from supper. All I have to do is dish out a plate for you."

"Okay," he said as he sat down. "If it's not too much trouble for you."

She brought the food and they talked together. She wasn't a gossip, but she had a great knowledge of the White House and the personnel who worked there. "I think you should know something that might be of importance to you," she said.

"What's that?" he queried.

"There is a great division between the personnel who have been here for some time and the new ones who have come. I won't tell you which is which. I'm sure you can get a list. But see if you can tell just by looking."

"I'll do that," he said. "The security of this place is part of my job."

"All of us guessed that," she said with a smile. "If there is any way I can be of help to you, just say so. By the way, I like your attitude. I feel we are on the same wave length."

"I feel the same way," replied Todd. Todd thought about that conversation he had had a few days ago and felt that he had two friends he could trust, Rusty and June. One had said, "I feel we identify with each other." The other had put it, "I feel we are on the same wave length." That made him decide that he would have supper with the kitchen crew. He had supper with them and joked around a bit. But June wasn't there. He had no trouble picking out the new and the old employees.

About eight o'clock in the evening, the President called and asked him to come to his office. Todd knocked on the door and was admitted by the President. No one else was present. Todd confessed to himself that he was nervous. How many nobodies get to see the President in person and have a conversation with him?

James Jackson was a handsome, middle-aged man with a friendly face. He seated Todd in a comfortable lounge chair, and sat down in another like it, facing the young man. After some talk about how Todd liked Washington, D.C. and whether he was comfortable in his apartment, Jackson changed his tone abruptly. "I suppose you wonder what you are doing here and why I have chosen you for this special job. You know that I chose you, don't you?"

"No, sir, I did not," the bodyguard replied. "However, I am deeply grateful that you did choose me, and I consider it a great honor."

"Well, let me explain that," said Jim Jackson as he leaned forward in his chair. "And by the way, relax and skip the formalities of title when we are alone. Call me Jim or Jackson. I haven't been President long, but already I am sick of titles when I am with people that I know, and I have to hear it all day. You are my bodyguard, but I need you as a companion and friend. There may be plenty of times at night when I may want to talk to you to see what John Q. Public is thinking out there, or just to let off steam to someone."

"I would like some informality," Todd agreed, "but it will be something I will have to get used to. Not everyone has the opportunity to see the President, let alone talk to him."

The older man smiled and went on with his explanation. "I got into politics early in life. My parents had great aspirations for me politically and knew the right people to launch me into it. First, in the state legislature and then in the United States Senate. My father and mother traveled a lot and left me with the grandparents, my mother's parents. Granddad was a farmer and a very religious man. My parents were not much on church and religion, which was a grief to my grandfather. So my granddad spent time with me talking about the Bible and the fact that he was a Christian. He wanted me to be one."

"As I got older, he could see that he wasn't getting very far with that, and he let up a little. I admired and respected him more than any man I ever met, and I still do. Even when I got into politics, I would go to see him from time to time. On one of these occasions I could see that his health was failing even though his mind was sharp and his eyes were clear. We sat at the kitchen table, and he said, 'Jim, I see that you are going places in politics. It wouldn't surprise me if you go right to the top and make the Presidency some day. I've been thinking about it, and I want you to make me a promise, okay?' He looked me right in the eye."

"I said, 'You mean that if I ever get to be President you want me to do something?'"

"He said, 'That's right.'"

"Well, at that time I had no aspirations to be President and considered that position beyond the realm of possibility, so I said, 'I promise. What do you want me to do?' Little did I know what was on his mind. He fingered his Bible, which was on the table, and read about two men. One was Daniel, who was the trusted right hand man of the king. The other was Joseph, who was second in command to the king of Egypt. He told me these kings owed their success to these men who worshipped God. 'What does this have to do with a promise?' I asked my grandfather."

"Then Grandfather said, 'When you are in office and need a bodyguard or right hand man, I want you to promise me you will choose a Christian. Promise me you will do that.'"

"The request took me totally by surprise and seemed very strange, but I couldn't back out of my promise. So I affirmed it again. I returned to my home, and Grandfather died one week later. That promise has haunted me ever since." The President stood up and paced the floor nervously. "Does this make any sense to you, young man?"

"Yes, it does," replied Todd. "I understand perfectly."

The older man continued, "That cropped up in my mind during the campaign, and when I won the Presidency, I couldn't forget it. So, one of my first acts was to request a personal bodyguard who would live in the White House. I told the head of security that I wanted a hand in the selection of a man, and I wanted the resume of every new man in the Special Security group. I went through them one by one. When I came to yours, you stated that you were a Christian. In fact, that intrigued me because you were the only one who stated that in his resume. That was what I was looking for in order to keep my promise."

"Ordinarily, I would have crossed you off the list when I saw that, thinking you might be some kind of fanatic. But I knew my grandfather was no fanatic. I checked you out in every way possible: physically, mentally, morally, all through your schooling, church, family, and all the people who have worked with you here. They all say you are the best—the cream of the crop. I need someone I can trust implicitly and finally concluded that if you were like my grandfather, I could trust you."

"The dangers I face as President are tremendous. We won't go into them in detail now, but there are many people who think I owe them because they helped me win this election. Some of them come from groups that can be mean when crossed. I want you in this job with your eyes wide open, knowing that your life will be in just as much danger as mine. So, if you have any doubts, say so now."

Todd thought for a moment before he replied. "Thank you for your explanation and frank warning. I pray about all my decisions in life, and I believe God has placed me in this position. I am not afraid. My objective is to please God and protect your life. I will put your life before my own. You will have my complete loyalty. I am a Christian like your grandfather, and you can trust me to always tell you the truth and be of help to you in any way day or night."

Jackson walked over to the desk, called a maid, and told her they were ready. She came in immediately with coffee and rolls and then was gone. "Do you drink coffee?" Jackson asked.

"Yes, I take my coffee black."

Seated once again with coffee mug in hand, the President resumed his talk. "You are going to know a lot about me that not many people know. I must have complete confidence that none of my private life or the life of my family or the inner workings of the White House will ever be revealed by you as long as I am alive. Do I have that promise?"

"You have it, sir."

Jackson continued, "You will be with me most of the time when I am out of the White House. However, whether I'm traveling or here at home, there may be times when I want to talk with you about almost anything. It gets lonely in politics, and I want not only a bodyguard, I want a friend as well. I am not a Christian. I have a philosophy that religion and politics don't mix. If I feel like talking about it, I'll let you know. Understand?"

"I understand," Todd said, "But I suspect that the subject may come up in many ways."

Jackson ignored that comment, absorbed with his own thoughts as he said, "I hate to say this, but one of your jobs may be to babysit me—to keep me out of trouble. I have two weaknesses that could blow my reputation. One is my temper, and the other is alcohol. When I get mad, I tend to say things I should not say. The media has a field day when I slip like that. I am not an alcoholic, and seldom do I drink. But when I do, it doesn't take much for me to go overboard. This can happen especially when I am traveling. I want you to watch me, and do your best to discreetly keep me from going too far. You have my permission. Head me off, divert me. My wife knows my problems and is a big help when she is with me, but I am alone many times. She tells me that if I had religion (she doesn't put it quite that way), I would get over these problems, but I doubt it. Ruth, my wife, says she is a Christian, but I don't know if she knows what she is talking about. I know Karen, her secretary, is one. She is always talking to Ruth about it."

Todd broke in at this point. "You can count on me to keep your secrets and to guard you from your weaknesses in any way that I can. It sounds to me like your wife is on the right track. I am looking forward to getting better acquainted with both her and Karen."

Jackson stood up. "We had better knock it off. I have a cabinet meeting at eight tomorrow morning." Todd took the cue and headed back to his apartment.

Chapter 4
The White House

The next few days were a blur of activity for the President. He was confined in his activities to the White House as Cabinet members were chosen and all the Special Interest Groups, who had helped him gain the Presidency, clamored for his attention and rewards. The papers were full of comments on his actions and choices of people to fill government posts.

During this time, Todd had the opportunity to survey the White House and its staff. About the only responsibility that claimed his time was keeping his appointments with his physical defense trainers. This occupied a part of every week when he was in Washington. His survey of the White House was an experience of learning the building from top to bottom. Jake Thurston was head of maintenance for the building. He had held that position for several administrations. He volunteered to be Todd's guide and gave him a course in history as well as making him familiar with the layout. He knew every room and closet in the building.

Todd made mental and written notes of personnel working in

the mansion. His primary interest was security, but he had a natural interest in people and their personalities. He had keen discernment and analysis of people and made note of special characteristics. Most of the people in the White House were unaware of his official business. Jake introduced him as the President's bodyguard and informed them that Todd would be living in the White House. This drew various reactions of warmth, nervousness, caution, friendliness and curiosity. Todd watched carefully each one, but responded in his usual friendly way, seeking to put others at ease. Food Services drew his special attention, knowing how vital that area could be to security. His mind went back to food and wine tasters in the courts of the ancient kings.

One day he went on his own to the office of the President's wife and staff. Karen was at the receptionist's desk, and their eyes met as he entered. Todd admitted to himself that she was the main reason he had come to this area. The brief meeting they had when he first arrived at the White House impressed him with her beauty and poise, but he had sensed a depth of character and grace that made him search her out again. Her eyes did not flinch as she greeted him with a warm smile.

"How nice of you to pay us a visit," she said warmly. "Are you looking for Mrs. Jackson?"

"To tell you the truth," he replied, "I am not here on any official business. But I was hoping I would see the President's wife, and . . . I hoped I would see you," he finished with a laugh.

Karen did not blush nor was she embarrassed as she joined in his laugh and quipped, "Well, that's the nicest thing I've heard today, especially coming from a bodyguard."

"How did you know I am a bodyguard?" he asked. "I haven't had much opportunity for official introductions in the White House."

"Most everyone in this place knows about you and what you are doing here. In fact, your presence makes some people downright nervous."

"Why is that?" he queried. "Do I make you nervous?"

"Of course not," Karen smiled. "But some become very self-conscious. Like when a police car is behind them in traffic."

"But I'm not a policeman," he said. "I am here to protect the President and look after his welfare."

"That's just it," she teased. "Your presence and responsibility makes us all suspect. Have you ever been in a department store, knowing that those hidden cameras are watching your every move? Even though you are honest and would not steal for anything, you are super conscious that someone might suspect you?"

"I understand," Todd said agreeably. "I have had that feeling, but I'll do my best to avoid giving that impression, especially with you. I see nothing about you that looks suspicious, in fact, quite the contrary," he ended with a disarming laugh. "I understand from the President that you are in about the same relationship with the President's wife that I am with the President."

"Well, not exactly," Karen laughed. "I shield her from people and am her confidant and personal secretary. I guess I would do my best to protect her in any way necessary," her voice trailed off.

Todd broke in, "From what I have heard from Rusty and others, you are very capable in martial arts and firearms in spite of your kind and gracious, and may I say, beautiful appearance."

This time Karen blushed. "Don't believe everything you hear. Appearance can be deceiving."

Just then an office door opened, and a lady came toward them. As she came, she spoke. "Todd, it's good to see you."

As they shook hands, Todd said, "I'm surprised you recognized me and knew my name."

"We met briefly a few days ago," Mrs. Jackson said, "and believe it or not, I know a lot more about you than you do about me."

This brought a puzzled look to Todd's face. "I don't understand," he said, looking intently from one lady to the other.

"Todd, do you have some time to chat with us?" Ruth asked.

"Why sure," he replied. "I'm free for the afternoon, and it would be a pleasure to get better acquainted."

The older lady nodded to Karen. "You take Todd into my office and wait there. I want you in on our conversation."

"Jennie," she called to a middle-aged lady with a rather stern face, seated at a desk out of normal ear shot from the receptionist's desk. "Take over the reception desk for the afternoon. I will be tied up for some time. No calls, no visitors."

"Will do," said Jennie in a loud voice, rising and making her way over to Karen's desk. Sitting down, she watched the man and two women enter Ruth's office, and then rather furtively, constantly watching that office door, she dialed a number and spoke quietly into the phone.

The office that Mrs. Jackson called her own was beautifully furnished and commodious. It was a combination of office with desk and living room with comfortable chairs. Todd noted that Ruth was about fifty years of age, dignified and refined, but not stiff. She was attractive, but not gaudy in any way. She was self-assured and intelligent, while at the same time having a gracious, motherly manner.

She reminded Todd a little of his mother and also the kind of woman he visualized Karen would be when she reached the age of Ruth. He was instantly at ease in the presence of both women, while at the same time wondering if this was really happening to him, actually sitting in the President's wife's office as though they were old friends.

Ruth broke the silence. "How about an afternoon snack?" she asked. Karen and Todd nodded their approval, and Ruth rang a bell for service. A young lady appeared through another door than the one by which they had entered. Ruth gave the order and when the girl left, closing the door, she began, "Call me Ruth. That makes it easier to carry on a conversation. We, Karen and I, have been wanting to talk to you ever since you arrived. This opportunity is just right for us. Karen is more than a secretary to me. She is a friend. My best friend and confidant."

Todd was thoroughly mystified by all these words, and it showed on his face. "Let me tell you what I meant when I said I knew more about you than you do about me," Ruth continued. "Karen and I have read your resume. My husband made available to me all the research by the FBI, your whole life and background. Karen and I have mastered it all."

"Why would you want to know so much about a nobody like me?" Todd queried, increasingly mystified.

Ruth went on. "We know your family background, your schooling from kindergarten on up, your college days, your athletic history, and all the details of your conversations with my husband. Best of all, we know you are a Christian. We want you to know that Karen and I are both Christians. Karen led me to the Lord not long ago, and a great change has taken place in my life. We are both praying for my husband. He told you about his problems, and we are so glad that he likes and has confidence in you. He wonders about me yet because he knows about my past real well. But I am growing so much, and Christ means everything to me."

"She is," Karen affirmed with a smile.

At this point a knock came at the door, and a girl appeared pushing a cart amply filled with more than a snack. The girl left, Karen gave thanks, and they began eating. The face of Ruth sobered as she began talking again. "I am concerned about my husband's safety, Todd. He carried a lot of political baggage into the office of President that he knew little about. He was backed by a whole array of special interest groups, some of whom could pose much more danger to him than the people in the party he defeated. He now realizes that if he doesn't play ball with those who helped put him in office, they could become very nasty and dangerous. In fact," her voice became hushed and earnest, "We know that there is a conspiracy to use my husband to make great changes in our government."

"Like what?" Todd queried.

"That's a long story," Karen broke in. "I know that the thought must go through your mind that these are just the fantasies of a couple of neurotic women who have been watching too many soap operas on television. Let me give you a little more background. You see, we were in Washington three months before the inauguration of President Jackson. During that time, swarms of people descended on the President with advice, plans, and threats."

"Gradually, out of that throng we began to detect an organized group of powerful people. Among them were senators, representatives, judges, military men, educators, etc."

"This group was largely responsible for planning, pulling strings, and raising finances for the campaign that put Mr. Jackson in the White House."

"They headed up a network of people that extended throughout the nation. This group also visualized the President and Vice-president to be puppets in their hands to achieve their goals."

"The self-chosen leader of this political organization is Mike Burly, who was once a union boss but was thrown out of the union because of strong arm tactics and misappropriation of funds. He has ambitions and methods that his honest backers know little about. Neither are they aware of his small core of men who do his bidding who are actually gangsters."

"Burly knows of and uses to advantage the tension and upheaval in Washington and the nation. However, he is portrayed by the media as a champion of the people and a great man."

"The head of the FBI knows that Burly is a scoundrel and somehow linked with the underworld which has been responsible for muggings and assassinations in the Washington area. He has warned the President to be on his guard about Burly and about the President's own safety. Patton, head of the FBI, has not been able to get the evidence he needs to expose Burly."

"President Jackson is greatly concerned because of the backing Burly has from good men who are completely fooled by the sweet words and seemingly gracious manner of this clever scoundrel."

"We are frightened, as well, not only by what we have told you, but by other things we have learned. Hence, we have looked and prayed for someone close to us that we could trust, with whom we could share these fears and information. We feel that you are that person."

Todd, dumfounded, started to speak, but Karen beckoned him to let her finish.

"We are just two women, scared half to death, carrying information that could involve the fate of a nation, knowing that probably no one will believe us. Then, you, Todd, came into the picture, and here we are spilling it all out into your ears. We believe we know you, but we know that we are taking a chance with someone we just met. We take the chance that you will not believe us, and the chance that you are a fake and a plant. However, at this point, we have no alternative. If you are a fake — we are sunk."

The pathetic and forlorn look on both women's faces touched Todd deeply. For all the physical prowess that he possessed and strength and confidence that he exuded, he was very tender. He felt their burden and fear deeply. "Ladies," he began, "I don't know what I can say to reassure you, but I do believe you, and I want you to know that I have no secrets. I am a plain American boy from a hard working Christian family. I have no political experience. I am not a fraud or a plant. I am thoroughly committed to the Constitution of the United States and to our form of government. I keep abreast of the news, and I love American history. I am also wise to forces that would like to undermine our government. I did not know the information that you confided in me, but I appreciate it and will join forces with you. I will not betray the confidence you have placed in me as we work together."

Relief showed visibly on the faces of the two ladies. "There are two other things I must tell you," Ruth spoke firmly. "One has to do with the security of the White House. Did you know that there has been no background check on the White House staff and personnel? And there are many new people. Mike Burly, head of the party, chose most of them, and he himself is suspect. That disturbs me."

"No, I didn't know that," Todd said. "But I will certainly see to it that it is done immediately if the President gives me the go ahead."

"Oh, that relieves me so much," Ruth murmured. Then she continued, "The second thing you need to know is that there is another group in Washington, made up of important and powerful people that is organized to expose and resist what the first group is trying to do. We don't know the personnel in either group. We can only guess. You can understand that neither group would trust us because of our place near the President. However, we do know one man who is a Christian who is part of the second group and made us aware of its existence. We have not told him all that we know. He knows of our stand, however, and he has warned us to be careful. Any action taken to expose any part of their plan or personnel by anyone can make that person a target. There have been several so-called mysterious accidents in Washington."

"I was just thinking, Todd. If you initiate a background check on personnel in the White House, you may become a target. We would not like that. Perhaps you had better leave it alone."

"Don't worry," he said. "I will be careful, but I know it must be done."

Karen spoke, "By the way, Todd, the Christian that Ruth spoke of knows of your position here and all about your background. He wants to meet you. He attends the little church where we go to Bible class on Wednesday nights. Would you like to go? You could meet him."

"If I'm free, I'll go," he replied.

"Todd," Karen said gravely, laying her hand on his arm, "now I'm worried about you. Maybe we shouldn't have involved you at all. If the subversive group even suspects that you might influence the President against them, your life will be in danger."

"Don't worry," the young man replied soberly. "Sooner or later I would have been involved. I told the President that I would lay down my life to protect his, and I will do all I can to protect my country as well. I'll let you know about tomorrow night. If you need me for anything, day or night, just call."

"I think we have done enough for now," Ruth said, somewhat relieved. "Let's break up."

With that, they parted. Todd gave Jenny a closer look as he went past the receptionist's desk. He stopped and asked, just to be friendly, "Nice to meet you, Jennie. How long have you worked here?"

She stammered as she replied, "I – I came three weeks ago." She would not look at Todd.

Todd was a marked man from that moment.

He mused, does she look guilty about something or is she just embarrassed? There was something about her manner that troubled him, especially after the conversation that he just had. "Have a nice day," he said as he went his way.

Reaching his apartment, Todd called the President on their special line. "I've been going through the White House, and I wondered whether a background check has been made on all personnel?"

"No, that has never been done with new personnel," said the President. "My advisors did not feel that was necessary inasmuch as they were hand-picked by them."

"It should be done immediately, Mr. President. We can't take that chance. Will you give me permission to ask the FBI to do it?"

"Of course, I will. You see to it. I will put it in writing, and you can pick it up immediately," the President answered.

"Thank you, sir. I'll take care of it." Todd picked up the telephone a few minutes later, called the proper department and delivered the President's order to verify it in person.

Within minutes, someone from the department placed a call to one of the members of the subversive committee with the information that Todd Bradley had ordered a background check on the White House personnel.

Chapter 5
Politics or Principles

Todd decided to skip supper because of his afternoon lunch. He stretched out in a reclining chair and gave himself to deep thought. His life had changed from the simple matter of protecting the President to involvement in some pretty heavy intrigue. Something was going on in Washington that had tentacles that perhaps reached all over the country and might be right here in the White House. And here he was right in the middle of it.

He was not an overly suspicious person by nature. He had been brought up among people he could trust, but he was far from naive. He had rubbed shoulders with a variety of people in high school and college. Living in college dormitories threw him in contact with the good and the bad. There was often cheating, thievery, fighting, drugs, alcohol, and deception of every kind.

His reputation for clean living, honesty, and good judgment, along with his physical prowess, landed him a job as a dormitory monitor and leader for three years of his college life and provided for his room and board. In that position he dealt with all kinds of problems, and he saw the dark side of people. He was detective, counselor, judge, and jury with the fellow students of his dormitory. In addition, his training for his present position impressed upon him the importance of noticing small details, the danger of overlooking telltale signs and the wisdom of analyzing people very carefully. This only sharpened his natural ability to read people.

The lady, Jennie, in the office of the President's wife troubled his thoughts. Was he being overly suspicious, or should her responses alert him to something? He jumped out of his chair and called Karen in her room. After a short greeting, he asked, "Karen, is there a record of every telephone call that goes out of your office each day?"

"Yes," she replied.

"Can you find out whether Jennie made a call from your desk this afternoon, and if so, to what phone she made that call?"

Mystified, Karen answered affirmatively to both questions and asserted she would check it out and call him right back. Ten minutes later she called. "Jennie made one call. Here is the number." She rattled off a series of digits. "It is to someone in the FBI department. Todd, what are you thinking?"

"Probably the same as you, Karen. I think she is a plant in your office and reported our meeting this afternoon to someone. Somehow, I didn't feel just right about her, and that call convinces me that my feelings were right. Don't let on that you have any suspicions, but inform Ruth and be on your guard. Keep her away from any sensitive material. She may prove to be useful to us. I'll try to see you tomorrow. Thanks a lot," Todd said and hung up.

"Well, Todd," he mused to himself. "Put that together with the fact that you ordered a check on the White House personnel today and that Bo dislikes you very much, and you are not very popular all of a sudden."

The telephone rang. It was the President. "I need to talk to you, Todd. Could you come to my office in about an hour?"

"I'll be there," Todd said, wondering immediately if this meeting would have anything to do with the events of the afternoon.

Knowing he had an hour, he decided to go to Food Service and see if June was there. Supper was over, and June was supervising the clean up and dish washing crew.

"Want something to eat?" she asked.

"No, but I would take a cup of coffee," he replied. "Do you have time to have one with me?"

"Sit down at a table, and I'll bring us both one," she replied.

"How has it been going down here?" He asked.

"Just fine. Have you figured out who's new and who's old around here? she asked as she smiled.

"You were right," he came back. "It's not hard to tell. I have a question, June. Are you acquainted with a new lady named Jennie who works in the President's wife's office?"

"A little," June responded. "She comes in here to eat some, and we've talked quite a bit."

"What is she like? How do you read her?" Todd pressed.

"Well, I know she is not married, at least not now, and never has been. I know she seems depressed most of the time and feels sorry for herself. I know she has wanted to get together with me, but I have been too busy. Besides, I start to get depressed when I'm with her too long."

"Do you know anything about her background or how she got here?" Todd asked.

"I know that she is one of the people that Mike Burly brought in, and that's about it."

"Thanks, June," he said as they both finished their coffee. "I have an appointment with the President in five minutes. See you again soon."

With that he jumped up, stopped at his apartment to get his briefcase, and went to the President's office.

The President invited him in and seated him. "I heard that you visited the ladies today. My wife told me," Jim said with a smile.

"I did," the young man replied. "I found both of them very charming. They spoke well of you."

"I'm glad you are getting acquainted." Jim said slyly, "I wouldn't blame you if you took a personal interest in Karen. She's a great young lady."

Todd laughed and exclaimed, "You might have something there. I suppose, however, that she might have an interest in someone else."

"Not that I know anything about," the President said. "However, let's change the subject. I've been getting a little flack on the background check of White House personnel."

Todd's face showed no emotion. "Is that right? Where's the flack coming from?"

"That is what puzzles me, both the flack and the source of it. Little complaint that I know of has come from the White House, but the knowledge of this has spread like wild fire among the people who backed me in the election campaign, plus the Attorney General's office. I would think that office would be the first to applaud the move."

"My sentiments exactly," agreed Todd. "Perhaps they have something to hide."

"Well, don't worry about it. We called for the check, and I'll feel better once it's completed. It has roused my curiosity, and now that I look back on it, I can't understand why that routine wasn't carried out. However, that's not the reason I asked you to meet with me. I told you previously that there would be times when I would want to bounce some thoughts and problems and ideas off of you. That time is here. I have a decision to make, and I'm all up in the air. I feel like getting drunk and forgetting the whole thing," the President said with a sigh as he poured himself a cup of coffee.

"That wouldn't do a bit of good and would only complicate matters. Let's get on with the problem," Todd said.

The President began pacing the floor as he said, "Have you been reading about the child abuse problem and the controversy that is raging across the country and in Congress?" He stopped, and Todd nodded his head affirmatively. Then he went on. "Well, Congress has just passed a law by a slim margin in the House and by three votes in the Senate called the Child Abuse Law. It is on my desk to sign into law, and I don't know what to do. This was triggered by a few dramatic cases of child beating across the country, almost all of them by drunken fathers or mothers or drug related. The press has played them up, and some special interest groups have magnified them way beyond the facts. Congress has responded to pressure from these groups. If I don't sign this bill, I'm a dead duck as far as media is concerned. But there are some bad ramifications. Here are some of the statements in this bill:

1. Child abuse shall be regarded as a federal crime.
2. Spanking, slapping, switching, or using physical force against a child will be defined as child abuse.
3. Anyone in a position of authority, such as a teacher, counselor, minister, etc., caught teaching parents or others to use physical discipline, such as spanking, on a child will be declared guilty of teaching others to break the law and will be subject to fines or a jail sentence.
4. Parents found guilty of child abuse will have their children taken from them. The courts will decide whether this will be temporary or permanent.

He stopped his pacing and glared down into Todd's face. "You wouldn't believe the letters, faxes, phone calls, and telegrams that have come, pro and con, on this thing. I can't believe Congress could be so dumb as to pass it. And nobody would believe the pressure that is on me from my pals who supported my election along with the psychologists, social workers, and teacher's unions to give my okay to it. Whichever way I go on this one, I'm sunk. The leaders of the House and Senate have put pressure on me to sign it. Almost every member of my cabinet counseled me to sign it. I talked to my wife (all the big wigs would laugh me out of office if they knew that), and she told me not to sign it. And here I am talking to my bodyguard, of all people, to get his advice. What do you think, Todd?"

"Let me ask you a question, Jim," the young man responded.

"Do you want to do what is right, or do you want to do the thing that will benefit you the most politically?"

"Aren't they the same?" Jim shot back. Wasn't I elected to do what the people want, and don't I have to do whatever is necessary to stay in power and please the majority if I am to do any good?" He paused and then went on, "And who is to decide anyway what is right and what is wrong? Aren't we on the right side to protect those kids out there?"

"Jim, listen to me now, and see if I make sense," Todd said earnestly as he motioned the man to sit down before him. "I want to put two things into your thinking. First, the Constitution of the United States. I see some glaring errors in this bill. Their definition of child abuse is wrong. I'll explain under the second point.

B) This bill tramples on the freedom of every parent.

C) This bill denies the freedom of speech of teachers, ministers, and counselors in this country. Pass this bill, and you will fill the jails with good people and destroy countless homes.

Point two, who is the authority on what is right and wrong when it comes to the family and discipline of a child? The Authority is God, and the Book He has given to us as our guide is the Bible."

At this point the President started to speak, but Todd held up his hand. "Let me finish. The Bible points out the fact that the family unit is the basic unit of all society. As the family goes, the society and that nation go. God has established the husband and father as the head of the family. Not as a tyrant and dictator, but as one who is to love his wife and children. He is the head of the house, the one who is the authority figure and maintains order and disciplines according to the Word of God. The mother and wife stands beside him, and they love each other and train the children together. She especially exhibits grace and love toward the children and makes the house a home. The children should be taught to honor and respect and obey their parents. That often must be taught with physical discipline. Note that it is the lack of these ingredients in the home and in this country that is responsible for the crime and killing and drugs that plague our nation. Note also what the Bible says in Ephesians 6:1:"

"Children, obey your parents in the Lord for this is right. Honor thy father and mother, which is the first commandment with a promise. That it may be well with thee and thou mayest live long on the earth. And ye fathers, provoke not your children to wrath, but bring them up in the nurture and admonition of the Lord."

"The Book of Proverbs also has much to say about discipline:"

"He that spareth his rod hateth his son: but he that loveth him chasteneth him betimes."

19:18

"Chasten thy son while there is hope, and let not thy soul spare for his crying."

22:6

"Train up a child in the way he should go: and when he is old, he will not depart from it."

22:15

"Foolishness is bound in the heart of a child; but the rod of correction shall drive it far from him."

23:13,14

"Withhold not correction from the child: for if thou beatest him with the rod, he shall not die. Thou shalt beat him with the rod, and shalt deliver his soul from hell."

29:15,17

"The rod and reproof give wisdom: but a child left to himself bringeth his mother shame. Correct thy son, and he shall give thee rest; yea, he shall give delight unto thy soul."

"You see," Todd concluded, "the Bible definitely teaches the use of physical force in the training of a child if it is necessary. There is a proper type of rod or switch, and a proper place to apply it. It should never be done in anger and should be done because the parent loves the child enough to discipline. Discipline not only has a correct effect but also gives the child a sense of security, of belonging in the family. It should not be done in such a way as to damage the child, but it is intended to sting and bring pain without damage to the body. I value the spankings I received as a child. Jim, if you sign this bill you will be going absolutely contrary to the Word of God. If you obey God's Word, you will never be sorry even if eventually you are thrown out of office."

It was an impassioned plea on the part of the young man, and as he finished, he was astounded at the things he had said. It was as though he ignored completely the fact that he was talking to the President of the United States.

Jim did not move or utter a sound for at least three minutes. Both men sat with heads down, thinking their own thoughts. Finally, Jim broke the silence.

"Thank you, Todd. I know what I should do, but I'm not sure I have the courage to do it. I think we had better break up now."

"Could I pray before we part?" Todd asked.

"If you would like," was the reply.

Todd prayed briefly but to the point that the President would have the wisdom and courage to make the right choice. The two men shook hands and were about to part when Todd said, "It has always been dangerous, but please don't go anywhere outside the White House without me. The decisions you have been making and now must make will please some but make others very angry. We must be careful. I want to be at your side."

"Thanks. I'll be careful. Good night," Jim said softly.

Chapter 6
"An Oasis"

Todd rolled out of bed rather early the next day, fixed his own breakfast, and made his way to the gym for a workout with some of the other Special Forces men. They ran together, did stretching exercises, and calisthenics. Then they paired off for a variety of lessons in martial arts, wrestling, boxing, and weight lifting.

Todd had developed a special friendship with Ron Bassett, whose locker was next to his. They had a similar background in college wrestling, and Ron was a man of high principles and convictions. The gym was the place where they usually met, and after a workout, would sit down and talk over a bottle of pop.

Ron had no time for that this morning. As he combed his hair and was putting on his coat, he looked cautiously around. Speaking in a whisper, Ron said, "Watch out for yourself. You are in danger. I can't talk now." Quickly he left the locker room.

Todd thought over those words. He knew that Ron had much more contact with the other Special Service men than he, and figured that whatever Ron knew he had learned by overhearing a conversation or someone had told him something deliberately.

Todd had not talked for some time with his friend Rusty McGiddo, the boxing coach, so he went up to his office. Rusty was alone. "Have you seen this?" Rusty queried, handing him the morning paper. Todd stared at the headline: "President Jackson Vetoes Abuse Bill."

"Thank you, Lord," Todd said prayerfully.

"When you read that paper, you will pray more than that," Rusty said ruefully. "They are after Jackson's hide, calling him insensitive to children, friend of child abusers, a traitor to his party, and a menace in the White House. Then," Rusty continued, "because of the security check on the White House staff, they are blasting him for carrying on a witch hunt, cruelty to employees, and listening to bad advisors. You know who that last charge is aimed at, don't you? At you."

Todd was shocked. "What makes you say that?"

"Let me just say this," Rusty said. "Washington is one of the greatest gossip rings among government employees that can be found in the country. That is especially true if you are in the right places. I am one hundred percent approving of the two decisions Jackson made, but I know and others know he didn't make them alone. Gradually, the word is getting out that you must be a big influence on him."

"I can't deny that," Todd said, "but I must admit that I am surprised that he took my advice on the child abuse thing. He had a tremendous decision to make, whether it would be politics or principle. How glad I am he went with principles, but I know it could cost him a great deal."

"Todd, you don't know how big that cost might really be." Rusty grimaced as he slowly spoke each word. "Let me enlighten you about some things. There is a committee in Washington that does not like our government as it was formed and so constituted. They want a big government with control over people, with themselves in the saddle. There are a core of men in that committee that are ugly and dangerous, a committee within a committee."

"That core of people will stop at nothing, including murder, to achieve their goals. The dangerous part is that the larger committee includes several prominent and good men who have been duped by the hard core. They are part of the liberal party that put President Jackson in office, and their support is made up of special interest groups. The word is out that you are to be targeted. You must be very careful. However, you have friends, and I am one of them. You can count on me if you need me."

"I know that." Todd smiled as he held out his hand. "I'll take very seriously what you have said and will call on you if I need you."

"I'll keep my ears open and keep you informed," Rusty said very soberly.

Todd's mind was filled with many thoughts as he drove back to the White House. Was he having some kind of a dream? How did he get involved in such weighty matters? Are these people warning me that my life is in danger? he wondered to himself.

A scripture verse he had learned in high school days flashed across his mind: "*Be anxious for nothing, but in everything by prayer and supplication, with thanksgiving, let your requests be made known unto God. And the peace of God which passeth all understanding shall keep your heart and mind through Christ Jesus.*" Peace and assurance came to his mind that God would see him through whatever lay ahead.

One thing he knew for sure: God had placed him in his present position for a purpose, insignificant though he felt himself to be. Nevertheless, he felt he had come to his present place for important reasons in the eyes of God. His great concern right now was for President Jackson. By this time he must have been alerted to the criticism of the media. Had it made him regret his veto? Could he stand in the face of a drop in the polls as far as popularity was concerned?

Arriving at the White House, Todd headed for the office of the President. The office secretary responded in the affirmative that Jackson was alone and announced Todd's presence to the President. Todd hurried in. His first words were "I saw the newspapers this morning and was overjoyed at your veto but devastated by the headlines of the newspapers."

To the young man's relief, Jackson calmly smiled and said, "I saw them, but I'm not bothered at all. There are some terrific editorials favoring my decision, and there has been a deluge of telephone calls and faxes coming. Ninety percent of them favor my decision and commend me for my decision. Don't worry about a thing, Todd. I feel good about the whole matter."

Todd heaved a sigh of relief and said, "Have you heard from the FBI on their background check of our employees?"

"I just received it about an hour ago," Jackson said. "It is very revealing. I have a copy for you."

Todd scanned it quickly. The list had been arranged according to date when each employee had been hired. Those who had been with the White House staff for many years were listed first. They, as well as some of the more recent ones hired during the previous President's administration had all been screened carefully when they were hired. Those were about seventy-five percent of the staff, and Todd scanned them quickly. They were clean as to background.

The last twenty-five percent who were hired by Mike Burly, the head of the political party that had engineered the election of President Jackson, were a different matter. The list was loaded with ex-cons, drug users and pushers, people whose loyalty to America was questionable, belonging to all kinds of questionable fringe groups. Todd looked up, and the President was smiling. "Quite a bunch of derelicts, don't you think?"

Todd nodded. "How could anyone possibly place such a bunch of questionable characters in the White House?"

"Well, you will be interested to know that the FBI cleared them all out this morning and are in the process of replacing them with several former employees, who were fired when Burley took this upon himself, and some new applicants who have excellent credentials. That was all done by my orders."

"I was crazy to let Burley assume such power after the election. He thought he could get away with anything because the party was a majority in the House, close to that in the Senate, and a President under their thumb. Well, I hope to rectify a few things now that I'm getting a little backbone." Jim was pacing up and down the office as he finished his speech.

Suddenly, Todd remembered a previous engagement he had made. "This evening I promised to go to church with your wife and Karen for Wednesday Bible class," he said.

"Yes, they are planning on it, and I have made arrangements for cars and security," the older man answered.

Todd had begun to wonder whether they should call off going to the church in the light of the information he had received from Rusty. However, he knew that would involve much explanation, and he did not want to alarm the ladies at this point. "Tell your wife to give me a ring when they are ready to go tonight. I'll be ready," Todd spoke as he made his way to the door.

Todd ate supper with some of the kitchen employees and noticed a whole new spirit among them. They laughed with one another and were much freer to talk with him. Jake, the White House engineer, was there and sat next to Todd. "Notice anything different?" Jake queried.

"Yes," Todd responded. "What's going on?"

"They are all happy because the characters are gone. You have no idea the pressure that gang put on all of us. They brought us all under suspicion. You are their champion, and they are grateful," Jake whispered.

"How do they know that I did anything?" Todd asked.

"Word gets around a place like this, and you can count on all of us to be behind you," Jake answered.

Ruth called shortly after Todd got back to his apartment. He checked his gun, which was hidden by his coat, and made his way to the lobby. Two cars were waiting for them. They got into the first car, the ladies in the back seat and Todd in the front seat beside the driver, who was one of his Secret Service friends. Two men rode in the car behind them.

Arriving at the church, they found that security had already checked out the building. About one hundred people had gathered for the Bible class in the front of the building. Ruth and Karen were greeted by the pastor. "We would like to introduce you to my husband's personal bodyguard and our friend, Todd Bradley," Ruth said. "Todd, meet Pastor Armfield."

The men shook hands and greeted each other warmly. "Everyone around here calls me either Pete or Pastor Pete," the pastor joked.

Todd liked the man immediately. He judged him to be about sixty years of age, medium build, with a kindly face. He was a man who put others immediately at ease. "It's a pleasure to meet you, Pastor," Todd replied. "I've heard much about you from the ladies – all good."

"That's music to my ears," the pastor said, laughing. "Well, it's about time to start."

About a third of the congregation that met Sunday mornings attended Wednesday Bible class, so they gathered near the front of the church. The ladies led Todd to a seat in the front row. Several choruses and hymns were sung, giving opportunity in between for people to give testimonies as to their personal relationship with Christ. Todd turned around each time to see who was speaking.

Sometimes, people also made requests for prayer. A lady asked prayer for her parents in Indiana for they were elderly. A high school student asked prayer for his testimony in school. A housewife and mother asked prayer for guidance in caring for twelve-year-old twin boys. A well-dressed middle-aged man stood up and gave a fine testimony of what Christ had done for him and meant to him, and then asked prayer for guidance for his work in the Senate.

Karen whispered to Todd, "That is Senator Michael Curry. I want you to meet him after class."

Finally the pastor went to the pulpit and asked them to turn in their Bibles to the Book of Daniel. Then he announced his subject: "You Can Make a Difference." The title caught Todd's attention immediately. His thoughts that day, brought about by the circumstances and the information he had received, had made him examine his life and the turbulent situation in which he found himself.

His background had been so different than his life now. He was brought up in a fine yet simple family, lived in a small town, attended a little known church. Now, suddenly he found himself in the nation's capital, a bodyguard of the President, and a companion and confidante to the most powerful man in the world. Not only that, but he was in the middle of a political volcano that could erupt at any time. He was told that his own life was in danger, and that there were those who saw him as a threat to their political aspirations. Then comes a title "You Can Make a Difference" from a man who probably knew little about him.

Todd was a young man who wanted God's will for his life. He believed that nothing took place by accident. He prayed for God's will and God's leading. He remembered his parent's words to him as he left for college and again as he left to train for the nation's security.

"Son," they said, "all we want for you is God's will for your life. Give your life to Him, and He will use you in His place and time for His glory. You can make a difference somewhere because we dedicated you to God as a child."

Todd's eyes were glued to the pastor's face as he spoke about Daniel. The thrust of his message was that Daniel was among the Israelites who were captured by Nebuchadnezzar and brought back to Babylon. Daniel was a lad of about fifteen. Yet, he was devoted to God. The Bible says about Daniel, "He purposed in his heart that he would not defile himself...." Nebuchadnezzar ultimately made Daniel the most powerful man in his kingdom and the advisor to the king. In every case because Daniel was faithful to God.

The pastor's application to his audience was that no matter who we are, God has a place for us. If we will yield ourselves to

Him, we will make a difference in that circumstance and setting. Todd sensed that message was tailor made for him. His heart responded with the confidence that God would lead him and use him in the place where God had placed him.

The class was soon over, and Ruth and Karen tried to introduce Todd to all of their friends. Most of the people were gone before Karen and Todd had a moment to talk with one another. Ruth came, leading the Senator to them. "Todd, this is Senator Curry. I want you to meet him because he is an important figure in the battle to which we alerted you."

"I'm glad to meet you, Senator," Todd said, looking the senator over carefully as they shook hands. "I appreciated your testimony and your prayer request." He measured the man carefully as he did most people. The Senator was a short, stocky man, neatly dressed, in a business-like, matter-of-fact manner, with eyes that searched Todd's face very carefully.

"What about the matter Mrs. Jackson just mentioned?" Todd ventured.

Curry was a cautious man which was apparent by his answer. "I'd rather not talk about that here," he answered, "but I'm free all tomorrow morning starting about 8 o'clock, if Ruth will invite us to her office. Then the four of us can discuss matters over coffee. It will take all morning."

"That will be fine with me," Ruth responded. "My office does not open until 1 PM so no one will be there to interrupt us."

"I appreciate your discretion, Senator. I will clear it with the President, and if I am free, I will be there. If not, I will let you all know," replied Todd.

On the way out, Todd saw the pastor and thanked him for his encouraging words.

At the White House, Ruth went immediately to the President's quarters. Karen and Todd lingered in the lobby and then sat down in a small lounge where they could face each other.

"What did you think of our church and the service tonight?" Karen asked.

"I thought your church and pastor were great, and I thoroughly enjoyed the message. It was just right for me and my need at this time." They discussed the night's meeting for a time and then Todd broke in, "Will you think I am bold or impertinent if I ask you a personal question?"

"Of course not," she answered with a smile.

"I'll preface it with another question. Do you remember the first time I saw you and met you several weeks ago?"

"Yes, I do," she answered. "It was when we had the reception for the new security guards who had just been sworn in."

"That's right," he answered. "And I haven't been able to get you out of my mind since that time. Tell me, are you committed to anyone else?"

She blushed for a moment and then said, "I am not committed to anyone."

Todd gave a sigh of relief. "That's great to know. I'm not asking how you feel about me. I just had to know whether I was looking down a dead end road."

"I might ask you the same question," Karen said with a quizzical smile.

"Absolutely no one," he responded. "I hope now we can keep enjoying each other's company."

"Agreed," she echoed.

"Now I have to tell you something else," Todd said. "The information you and Ruth gave me when we met together has been preying on my mind. I am greatly concerned about the safety of you ladies. I was going to keep this from you because I did not want you to get alarmed, but I believe you should know." With that he proceeded to tell her of the two warnings that had come to him about his own danger.

"I am now convinced that anyone who is in a position where he or she could influence the President is in a place of danger. I am sure that God will care for us, but we must be very careful. You and Ruth could be prime targets." With those words, they parted and went to their apartments.

Chapter 7
"The Issue Clarified"

The four met again in Mrs. Jackson's office at the appointed time the next morning. They sat around a table with the men facing each other and the women likewise. The table was supplied with coffee, hot chocolate and an abundance of breakfast rolls.

After a few minutes of greeting and selecting rolls, Ruth said, "Senator, I don't know exactly what you are going to say but, knowing you, I am eager to listen."

Curry was a senior statesman in the Senate, probably the most respected man among the conservatives on the hill. His life and his record were without blemish, and he was noted for his integrity. Bccausc of his reputation and his fearlessness, his enemies had many times lied about him and tried to dig up some scandal that would tarnish his image. But none of this had ever worked. He remained a tower of conservative strength and virtue.

Though he was now elderly, people listened when he spoke. Todd sensed some of this as he sat across from the man. Curry spoke earnestly as a man greatly burdened. "Young man," he began,

"You may be wondering why I have taken enough interest in you to have a meeting such as this. And, as I continue, you may wonder why I would trust someone whom I met only last night."

"Those thoughts have crossed my mind," Todd answered. "In fact, my sleep was somewhat fitful last night. You know, my life, up until now, has been in a small town, country atmosphere. I haven't known many public figures other than the representative from our district who nominated me for the Security Force."

"Coming right to the point," the senator said, "Your position with the President has given us a glimmer of light that is beyond our imagination, especially because you are a Christian. The ladies told me that. How long have you been saved?"

"I was brought up in a Christian home and accepted Christ as my Savior when I was five years old. That was during family devotions. My Christian life was fortified by my home life and attendance at a Bible-believing and teaching church."

"Great!" Curry responded. "The ladies have also shared with me all of your background material including your staunch life for Christ through high school and college. You seem to be clean in every way."

"I am also aware of your diligence to see that new personnel in the White House had a background check. Along with all this, I respect the judgement of Ruth and Karen who highly recommend you."

Todd responded, "As I told them, my life is not complicated. What you see is exactly what I am. I come from a very conservative family, and I share the concern of my parents about our nation and its departure from God and the Bible and the resulting flood of sin that has inundated this country and resulted in foolish government decisions."

"You speak of some weighty responsibilities for me and perhaps some dangers."

"I can't stress that too much," the older man mused soberly. "Our very lives may be at stake."

"You are the third person in the last few days to warn me of that. Proceed, I'm anxious to hear what you have to say," Todd replied.

Curry sat back in his chair and sipped his coffee before he spoke. "Please bear with me as I review a little history of our country. Probably they all are things you know, but they are things that are being left out of schools' history books today."

"Modern, so-called historians are bent on students thinking of our nation from a wholly secular standpoint. They have been in complete control of the history books for over 30 years. God and the Bible do not exist in our nation's history as far as they are concerned."

"It may well be that the chaos that exists in our nation today is the judgment of God upon an ungodly people. What a horrible mess we are in! It may be as God said in the Bible in Romans 1:24-28 – '*Wherefore God also gave them up to uncleanness ... God gave them up unto vile affections ... God gave them over to a reprobate mind.*' In other words, God in effect says, 'All right, you think you can go on without Me, I'll let you do your own thing.' And this is the result."

"Having said this, however, I'm going to do all I can do, as long as I live, to get this country on the right course. That is why I look at God's wisdom in bringing Karen into the life of Ruth, hence Ruth's salvation, and now you, a Christian, the right-hand man of the President. Surely, God has something good to do at least for our particular time."

"Now, on with our history. God had His hand on the founders of our country in the Declaration of Independence, the formation of the Constitution, and the Bill of Rights. Let me quote briefly from some men:"

"Benjamin Franklin — 'In the beginning of the contest with Britain, when we were sensible of danger, we had daily prayers in this room for Divine protection ... Our prayers were graciously answered ... Have we forgotten this powerful Friend? Or do we imagine we no longer need His assistance ... The longer I live, the more convincing proofs I see of this truth: that God governs in the affairs of man. And if a sparrow cannot fall without His notice, is it probable that an empire can rise without His aid? ... I therefore beg leave to move, henceforth, prayers, imploring the assistance of heaven and its blessing on our deliberation be held in this assembly every morning.'"

As the Senator paused, Karen broke in with a question, "Senator, do you think it was the fear of the Founders that some day our nation might turn away from God?"

"By all means," he affirmed. "Listen to some of the warnings that they gave."

"George Washington – 'Reason and experience both forbid us to expect that national morality can prevail in EXCLUSION OF RELIGIOUS PRINCIPLE.'"

"James Madison – 'We have staked the whole future of American civilization, not on the power of government ... but upon the capacity of us to govern ourselves ACCORDING TO THE TEN COMMANDMENTS OF GOD.'"

"Noah Webster — 'The moral principles and precepts contained in the SCRIPTURES OUGHT TO FORM THE BASIS OF ALL OUR CIVIL CONSTITUTIONS AND LAWS. All the miseries and evils which men suffer from vice, crime, ambition, injustice, oppression, slavery, and war proceed from their DESPISING OR NEGLECTING THE PRECEPTS CONTAINED IN THE BIBLE.'"

Curry stood up, pushing his chair back from the table. "That's just a little of the warning our forefathers gave. Let's take a little break."

They all stood up, continuing the discussion with each other.

"Ruth," Todd questioned as he stood before her munching a roll he had in his left hand and balancing a cup in his right hand, "Does your husband ever talk about history and the things the Senator has been reviewing this morning? Does he ever seem to be thinking about his place today and whether God is working in any way?"

All eyes turned toward Ruth as they waited for an answer.

She thought a moment before she spoke. "You have to realize that Jim doesn't know yet what to make of me since I told him I was now a Christian. He is very kind, but he is watching me carefully to see if this is some kind of a fad which I will perhaps soon cast off. I don't always know what is going on in his mind."

"I do know, however, that he has told me he can't understand how the atheists got a strangle hold on the schools and that he wants to do something to correct that situation. I have been reading an old book that was published in 1983. Senator Curry gave it to me. The name of the book is, *'The Stealing of America,'* by John Whitehead.[1] The book compares the steps of Hitler and Germany toward a complete takeover of the government by Hitler with some steps the United States has taken. Such as, take over of the schools. Hitler declared Jews to be subhuman, hence it was legal and right to kill them. America has declared babies in the womb to be subhuman, hence it is legal and right to kill them. And the rise and power of government, etc. I left that book lying on the end-table in the living room, and I saw him reading it one evening. His comment was, 'This book is quite interesting. Where did you get it?' I told him that Senator Curry gave it to me. He didn't make further comment, but I left the book out there, and I have seen him reading it several times."

"That's encouraging," said Curry. "Let's continue our discussion at the table."

When they were again seated at the table, he continued. "With as few words as possible, I want to bring you up to date on conditions as I see them."

"In the early days of our country, education was in the hands of religious people. The great colleges in the east were started and run by Christians. They educated the teachers who taught in the primary and secondary schools, and the Bible was part of their training. Most of this was in one room school houses with multi grades."

"The time came, however, when the state took over with the phi-

---

[1] Crossway Books, Westchester, IL

losophy that it is the state that has the 'right' and the responsibility to educate the youth. The presence of the Bible and freedom to express the truths of the Bible and God continued in the public schools for a number of years until gradually secular humanism and evolution began to predominate."

"Although this was a new religion with man as his own god, or impersonal matter as god, and evolution was its explanation for how all things came about, the atheists disguised this fact and said that there was a wall of separation between the church and the state according to the Constitution and that the Bible and all statements about God were to be excluded from the school. That left the atheists free to teach their doctrine without any challenge by the truth."

"The lie that has been accepted and supported by the Supreme Court is first, that there is a wall of separation between the church and the state applying to schools. In fact, Congress was never to make a law prohibiting freedom of speech or the free exercise of religion. And second, it is a lie that atheism and evolution are not themselves religion. Atheism has as its impersonal god, matter, as the author of all life and things. Evolution is its process."

"Following that came the decision of the Supreme Court in the case of , *Roe v. Wade* which legalized abortion. Thus, the door was opened for the murder of millions of babies considered non-persons in the womb."

"This contributed to the devaluing of human life. Human life is cheap in this country today."

"You know the rest — crime, murder, lying, stealing, fear, unrest, sodomy, incest, and the list could go on and on. Many fear to leave their homes at night."

"Speaking of the value of human life," Todd broke in, "Did you hear the news this morning? Senator Custer was gunned down in his car last night while driving home from a committee meeting."

"I learned of it last night," Curry replied. "The assassin was caught along with the driver of the car involved in the shooting. I feel so bad for Custer's wife and children. Custer was a good man with high principles and integrity. He knew he was targeted just like I know that I'm targeted. I am so sorry that he was driving alone at night."

"That brings me to my main reason for suggesting this meeting this morning. There is a great battle going on in Washington right now that reaches out to the whole country. It is a battle on two levels. One, the combatants on the public level are the Creationists and the Humanists. Their differences are reflected in the way they look at the size of government, the handling of taxes and finances, the value of human life, homosexuality, the public schools, and our very form of government — whether to remain a representative Republic or become a Socialist state."

"James Madison stated the issues right at the beginning of this nation when he said: 'We have staked the whole future of American civilization, not on the power of government, far from it. We have staked the future of all of our political institution upon the capacity of each and all of us to govern ourselves, to control ourselves, according to the Ten Commandments of God.'"

"The old division of Republicans and Democrats is almost obliterated as Creationists and Humanists are found in both parties."

"Let me make it clear that not all Creationists are Christians, but they at least recognize the importance of recognizing God and the Bible in all areas of our nation."

"Likewise, not all who are in the Humanist camp are atheists. Some of them do not even know the meaning of humanist. Some well-meaning ones just think there is no place for any religion in our government."

"That is the first level. The very public level, often people on both sides who are not well informed concerning issues and often vote concerning their personal material desires."

"Secondly, there are the combatants on the secret, inside, planning levels. You have to understand that our nation is in a dangerous situation. The whole nation is on the verge of anarchy. People are hungry. Gangs are forming and are dangerous. Lawlessness is increasing. The time is ripe when some group might try to take over the government."

"The Humanists have an inner core of people, called the Committee, who plan and orchestrate everything. The upper level of humanists are completely in the dark as to the plans of the Committee. It was the Committee who planned the choosing of Jim Jackson to run for President, and Archie Cornwall for Vice-President. Both men had been in the political arena and both seemed to lean toward the Humanist viewpoint and appeared to be electable. Both were low-key and noncommittal on issues, and that seemed to fit the mood of the country."

"Jackson especially was well liked by his colleagues and was not known for making waves in Congress. Cornwall was just considered to be a chubby politician."

"The Committee was headed up by Jack Burly who was low-key as far as the public was concerned, but dominated the Committee. He had plenty of experience behind him as a former union boss and had been involved in shady deals as he manipulated his way to the top of his union. In that position he came to know unprincipled politicians. His union finally got wise to his crooked ways and threw him out of office."

"He joined forces with politicians who chose him to lead the Committee. Soon he was in full control of the committee, a group of highly questionable people."

"The front of the Committee, however, was made up of men who presented a respectable appearance, and they knew others who were prominent in government."

"Burly planned a clever campaign for the election of Jackson and Cornwall while he remained out of sight throughout the campaign."

"When Jackson and Cornwall won the Presidency and Vice-presidency, the Humanists were elated. The Committee felt they had the government and power in their grasp. The President and Vice-President were to be merely figure heads in the hands of the Committee."

"Now let me digress for a moment and tell you about the inner core of the Creationists. Some of us became aware of Burley and his Committee and also of their plans to take over the government, hopefully by winning an election and declaring a national emergency by means of the President who would call for martial law which they would never end. But if they lost the election, they were geared to take over the government by force."

"So, in opposition to this group, we formed a committee of thirty top men in our government, god-fearing men, who have only two goals: first, to stop any subversive attempt to take over the government by force. Second, to use Constitutional means to bring our nation back to the place where we have freedom of religion, not 'from religion,' or prohibiting the free exercise thereof."

"These two committees, or groups to which I have referred, are aware of one another's existence. However, Washington at large knows little about them."

"Our committee, the Creationists, has a central core of four people, of whom I am the Chairman. The other three are Archie Cornwall, the Vice-President, Chuck Patton, Head of the FBI, and General Bruce Smith, highest ranking man in the military."

"I must admit that when we lost the election we felt like this was the end. We were whipped. However, since we have learned of you three people, the whole picture is changed."

"Well, now you know it," the Senator said with a sigh of relief as he looked at Todd. "What do you think of the situation?"

Todd toyed with his cup of cold coffee for a moment before he replied. "I confess that this is all news to me, but I am not shocked too much having observed the turmoil that swirls around this city the last few months. I assure you, Senator, I am with you all the way. My first responsibility is the safety of the President and his wife and Karen, but you can count on me to stand with you. I fear for you, too, Senator. Can I take you back to your office?"

"That won't be necessary, Todd," Ruth spoke. "I made arrangements, through the President, for his protection over here and back to his office."

"One further word, Todd," Curry said as he stood to go. "I hope this is not too sudden, but we have a meeting of our committee two weeks from tonight. Could you possibly meet with us? I would like you there to meet the men."

Without hesitation Todd replied, "I will be there unless the President needs me."

"The time will be 8 PM on the 12th Floor of the Knickerbocker Hotel. It is the Council Room, 1201. I will inform my core committee that you are coming," said the Senator. He arose quickly, expressed his appreciation to all, and then he turned and addressed Todd again. "Remember Custer and be very careful. You are undoubtedly a marked man." And with that, he left.

Todd sat very quietly for a time while the ladies waited for some response from him. "I don't fear for myself," he broke the silence, "But I do fear for you two and the President. This is almost too overwhelming for me to take in."

"You know, the enemy could be anywhere, even in the White House. Please don't leave the White House without telling me."

"We will do the best we can to be careful," Ruth answered. "This is a time when we must trust the Lord."

Todd prayed and then quickly left the office. As he went through the office, his glance fell on Jennie's desk. He mused, "I wonder what part she is playing in this grand scheme of things."

Chapter 8
"Crisis"

Several days went by with Todd's time divided between workouts in the gym, being at the President's side whenever he left the White House, and planning some event with Karen every day or evening.

Today, President Jackson had an early meeting with leaders of the House and Senate in the Senate Building. Todd was at his side until he went into the room where the meeting was held.

Todd seated himself in one of the lounge chairs in the hall that served as waiting room. He was browsing through a magazine when he looked up to see the Vice-President, Archie Cornwall, who had greeted Todd by his first name.

"Good morning, sir," he said with a smile as he respectfully stood up.

Cornwall was a short, rotund man with a big round face and double chin. His head was bald except for a few hairs which he had nursed to grow long from the side of his head and which stretched across the bald area. It was a feeble attempt to cover the bald spot, and a disaster when he got caught in a wind. His face seemed always to break out into a smile.

Archie reached up to put his hand on Todd's shoulder. His bodyguard looked on. "Nice work, young man," he said.

"What do you mean?" Todd questioned.

"I mean you are just right for the President. He is showing a lot more confidence. His last veto was great, and you are doing a great job securing the White House. Keep up the good work."

"You give me much more credit than I deserve, sir. The President is his own man," the younger man replied.

"Yes, yes, you are right," spoke Archie with the big, ready smile. "Well, I'm late for the meeting. See you later." With that he entered the committee room.

Both of the bodyguards were acquainted with each other. They had spent much time together in training.

"How do you like your assignment with the Vice-President, Pete?" Todd ventured.

Pete answered, "Oh, it gets a little boring at times, but when we're on the street, it is rather scary with all the kooks that are around. That keeps me on my toes. It seems like whenever we go outside there are people standing around who hate anything that looks like government. The Vice-President doesn't make life easy for me because he is so careless. We have had several close calls."

They both sat down and Pete said, "How's it going in the White House? I wouldn't mind being over there within eye shot of that beautiful secretary of the President's wife. I understand by the grapevine that you have an interest in her."

"I would say that it is easy to have an interest in her. She is a great young lady. However, don't put too much stock in the White House grapevine. I'll keep you informed of any concrete progress," Todd spoke with a laugh.

"It sounds like you stirred up a hornet's nest over the White House background check that you initiated," Pete said. "I don't know how it all came about, but the news media lay the praise or blame on your shoulders."

"That is somewhat of a conundrum, Pete. I'm not a public figure to the news people. Someone from inside of the government must have done some talking to the media."

"I don't know whether you know a guy by the name of Jack Burly, Todd, but he is a politician, an insider, who packs a lot of wallop in the government. He has made it known that he hates you with a passion. Somehow he knows everything that goes on in the government. Your background check helped get rid of people he had placed in the White House. He has contacts with some news buddies and probably is responsible for the news leak. By the way, he is a close buddy of Bo Campbell, the guy you humiliated on the wrestling mat. I have seen them together several times in Al's Coffee Shop where many of the fellows meet to have coffee and to talk. That's the best place in Washington to get the inside news on government people."

Todd listened carefully. He had sat next to Pete in classes during training and they had become friends, but he had never heard him talk so freely. He wondered if Pete was trying to warn him about something.

"That's all interesting, Pete, but I'll try to stay out of the limelight in the future if I possibly can," Todd said.

Pete yawned, "I'm going to walk around and stretch my legs a bit. I hope that meeting will end soon."

Todd was left alone with his thoughts. He wondered what kind of man Archie Cornwall was. He had met him on two different occasions. The first was at a social function where the President and Vice-President met with a group of lobbyists. The alcohol flowed quite freely, and for the first time Todd saw the President imbibe. Todd saw his chance to get alone with the President and whispered to him that he had had enough and that Todd would bring him coffee. Jackson acquiesced, and the bodyguard removed the wine glass and brought coffee as though it had been requested by the President.

At that occasion, the Vice-President imbibed quite freely and made a special effort to see Todd and sing the praises of President

Jackson. It all sounded rather phony, as Todd recalled.

The other occasion was at a welcome for the Prime Minister of Great Britain. The Vice-President introduced his wife to Todd. She was a pleasant lady, and they seemed well matched.

The President and Vice-President had known each other for many years, having been in the Senate together. It was well known that Archie was very loyal to the President and backed him up on every issue of government.

Todd mused over his conversation with the Vice-President today and how quickly Archie agreed with Todd when he had just stated the opposite thought. His thoughts focused on the name Archibald Cornwall and how the name and shape fitted a politician perfectly. He smiled at the mental picture.

Karen had said the Vice-President held her hand too long when she was introduced to him. That caused questions in her mind. The thought reminded Todd that he would like to hold her hand sometime. As far as Archie was concerned, Todd figured him to be harmless and pretty much a policy man and man pleaser, going whichever way the political wind blew.

What about the statements of Pete today? Why would a big shot like Burly have any interest in Bo? What could they possibly have in common?

The door to the committee room suddenly opened and Todd's random thoughts ended. He was all business as the President and Vice-President appeared.

Pete joined him as they escorted their charges toward the door at the end of the hall and lounge. Several security men appeared to clear and guard the way to the waiting cars.

With the President once again escorted safely to the White House, Todd headed for the office of the President's wife. Jennie was there, and he greeted her with a smile and "Good morning." She was nervous immediately but managed a smile and a greeting. Todd decided that he would engage her in conversation.

"Jennie, how is your day going?"

"Busy, but it's going all right," she responded.

"Do you live in Washington?"

"No, I have an apartment in Arlington."

"Your accent sounds like you were brought up in Kentucky, right?"

"Right. That is where my parents lived."

"How long have you lived in the Washington area?"

"A couple of years."

"You must know a lot of people and have a lot of friends in this area by this time." Todd noticed hesitancy on her part to answer this question, like she might be afraid he had checked her background.

"Well,...I have made a few friends, but I don't have much social life."

"Karen and I will have to change that for you and take you out with us. Would you like that?"

"I...I don't know how that would work. I would just be in the way."

"Nonsense," said Todd. "You think about it and we'll keep it in mind. See you later. Nice talking with you." Todd turned away and headed for Karen's desk.

"Are you busy?" he quipped.

"I certainly am, but not too busy," Karen said with a toss of her head. "What can I do for you?" she beamed at him.

"How about an early lunch with me?" he asked.

"Well, I think that can be arranged. Let me see what Mrs. Jackson says." She hurried off into Ruth's office and returned in seconds.

"Take over, will you, Jennie?" she called.

Jennie nodded her acceptance, and Karen took Todd's arm as they went out.

"Where to?" she asked.

"Wherever you say," he replied.

"Why don't we eat in my apartment? I have two frozen microwave dinners that can be ready in minutes," she spoke as she looked pertly up in his face.

"Great, sounds good to me."

"That was quite a conversation you had with Jennie," Karen spoke as a statement and a question.

"You're right. I wanted to be friendly with her, but I was fishing a little to see if she would get nervous. She did, I'll tell you more when we get to your apartment."

Her arm was still in his, and he reached up with his other arm and took her hand in his. "You know," he said, "I was thinking this morning how nice it would be to hold your hand. Do you mind?"

"Not at all," she said, smiling up into his face. "But it is going to take two hands to get my key out of my purse." He laughed and let her go ahead to unlock and open the door to her apartment.

Karen had two lunches in the microwave and the table set in record time. As they ate and looked at each other across the table, Karen's mood changed from light to somber. "You know Todd, I feel like we have known each other a long time, longer than the few weeks since Ruth and I laid a big problem on your shoulders. Are you nervous or scared about the meeting with Senator Curry's committee tonight?"

"Nervous, yes. Scared, no," he replied. "Maybe I will be more scared when I know more of the details of what I have gotten into. I'm surprised that you remembered that this is the night."

Karen's eyes dropped to her plate, and she looked very troubled. "That's all I've been able to think about since we met with the Senator. I know how serious this all is, thinking of what happened to Senator Custer, and I would feel terrible if something happened to you."

"Do you mean you would feel guilty and to blame because you gave me information which drew me into the problem?"

Her face flushed. "It's that all right, but more than that…" She looked up and he could see tears in her eyes.

"I admit that I have a personal interest in you, and I don't know what I would do if I lost you," she murmured, dabbing her eyes to hide the tears.

Todd left his chair and came around to her side, pulled her up to her feet and embraced her with his mouth next to her ear. "Those are the most wonderful words that I could ever hear," he whispered to her gently. "I'm so glad you feel that way about me because I've fallen like a ton for you. Please don't worry. I'm not careless or cocky about this danger, but it hurts me to see your apprehension and tears."

Todd longed to hug and kiss her at that moment, but he resisted that urge because he never wanted to take advantage of her emotions. Instead, he said, "I'm confident that God is leading in our lives and will take care of us. Trust Him and pray for me." He gave her a little hug and walked her back to her office area.

Todd might have been more concerned had he witnessed the meeting of the Humanist Committee two nights before. The committee members met in the basement room of a downtown restaurant. This was their regular private meeting place. The first part of the meeting was attended by the core committee and fifteen others who were never included in planning strategy, nor did they know the dark plans of Burly and his core committee.

Among the fifteen was a congressman, a judge, a general, a university professor, two wealthy businessmen, and several other prominent, respected government and former government men.

These were the front and available people of the committee if any question was asked about the composition of the group. They were committed to the idea that church and state should always be separated. Two of the men were out and out atheists, but most of the men were church goers to churches where the preaching content was mostly social issues with a minimum mention of the Bible.

These were also the men who were the contacts with congressmen and members of the Supreme Court and frequently the media.

Burly maintained contact with every one of them and kept several of his core group out of their sight for various reasons.

Jack Burly was an impressive looking man. He was a little over six feet tall and weighed two hundred and fifty pounds. He had huge hands which became very prominent when he was speaking. His hair and mustache were jet black. His complexion was somewhat swarthy. His eyes were dark and riveting, even sinister at times, and his emotions played quickly and noticeably across his face.

He moved around the room among the men just mentioned with ease. A smile played across his face and he spoke to each with friendliness and confidence. They like him. It was obvious to all that Mike Burly was in charge and they were anxious to hear what he had to say. They were all very pleased with the success of the Presidential campaign and gave Burly full credit. They fully expected the President and Vice-President to perform as the servants of their group.

Finally, they all took their places around a huge table, sipping their glasses, and looking expectantly at Burly. He began with, "I want to give you a little progress report. I trust that you are all encouraged by the sweeping victory we had in electing the President and Vice-President. Now we expect to expand that beachhead in achieving the goals we have in mind."

"Burly," the congressman called out. "What happened that the President didn't sign the bill we hammered out on child abuse? I thought we had him in our pocket."

This took Burly by surprise. A great quiet settled over the meeting, and Burly's face turned to fiery red, displaying either anger or embarrassment. He was not used to being challenged like this, especially at the beginning of a meeting and having his whole game plan upset.

"The President is in our pocket, but there are adjustments we must make and he must make before everything is in place. Just be patient until those adjustments are made. Our strategy calls for letting the opposition win one or two before we hit them with the big ones. Okay? Do you understand?"

Burly had regained his composure, his big smile of confidence reappeared.

"Okay, I understand," said the congressman as he settled back in his chair. Burly was far too intimidating to pursue something further, the congressman concluded.

Following this, Burly launched into his prepared speech on the achievements of the group, their basic purposes and his appreciation of their backing.

He emphasized very strongly their purpose to carry on in keeping with the Constitution of the United States, always with firm integrity. He lamented the mess the country was in and blamed the Creationists and their narrow views for every wrong; economically, morally and socially, be it at home or abroad.

There was no doubt about it. He had a way about him to inspire confidence and to fire them up about the great things they were going to accomplish.

After about thirty minutes of his oratory and rhetoric, he fielded a few questions and then dismissed the meeting. They departed rather quickly and the core group remained for their meeting.

A few others came in who did not want their identity known to the larger group. Among them was a man from the FBI department, and Bo Campbell, a security guard. Neither Bo nor the FBI man, Kurt Brenner, wanted their name or their work known to anyone except Burly. Two of the men who came in, only for the core group meeting, looked like gangsters or thugs. Only Burly knew their identities.

When they were all settled around a table, Burly came right to the main point of the meeting. "We have a problem that we didn't anticipate and that we must solve. We elected Jim Jackson as President and figured we could consider him as a figure head while we told him what to do. Everything looked great until a girl, who calls herself a Christian, became secretary to the President's wife, and now Mrs. Jackson says she is a Christian. To make matters worse, the President wanted a personal bodyguard and chose a security guy who claims to be a Christian. This guy is a bad influence on the President and could upset all our plans."

Burly gulped down some beer. "Any ideas from you?" He glared around the table.

"There have been plenty of accidents around Washington lately. Maybe he will have one," spoke one of the shady characters.

"Fortunately, we never stoop to such tactics," said Burly with a sly smile. "However, for sure we must come up with some way to get that bodyguard out of our hair before he wrecks everything."

The FBI man spoke up, "Washington is getting very suspicious about accidents. The assassination of Custer has stirred up a hornet's nest. I'm glad those actions are far removed from a group like ours." He looked around from face to face not expecting a response. "Look, we aren't getting anywhere. Why don't we just leave it in the hands of someone that Burly appoints. Not someone to do any job but can come up with a solution by parties unknown to us and unrelated to us who have the same ax to grind?"

Bo spoke up, "I second that motion. Sounds like a good idea. One thing is for sure, we are a nonviolent group."

Burly noticed the smirks on several faces as Bo finished. "Okay," he said, "We'll wait and see what will happen. Time to break up. Bo, stick around for a minute."

When all the men had filed out, Burly and Bo sat down across from one another.

"What are you thinking, Bo?"

"Why don't you let me take care of it, Jack? I won't do anything personally, but I have a pal who knows a couple of real pros who can scare him and put him out of commission for a few months or permanently. It will cost something, but it will be worth it."

"How much will it cost?"

"I'd say about $25,000. Can you lay hold of that in a hurry?"

"No problem. Charlie can get me the money any time. By the way, I have a contact who tells me that Todd is going to attend the meeting of the other committee tomorrow night at the Knickerbocher Hotel. It isn't often he is out of the White House alone. Can we work that fast?"

"We can if you can have the money tonight."

"I'll call right now and see if Charlie has it."

Burly called and was assured he could pick up the money immediately.

Before they finally separated, all plans had been made and all the contacts secured with complete identification of Todd given. Bo's final words to his contact were, "Remember, from this point on you don't know me and never heard of me."

Todd rested in the afternoon and had an early supper in the White House dining room with June Edison and Karen.

June had them laughing with some of her stories and for a while Todd's mind went from the meeting that night to enjoyment with his friends.

June soon left to meet with her kitchen crew, and Karen and Todd went to his apartment. Concern showed on Karen's face. "Somehow, I don't want you to go to that meeting, Todd. That will put you on the front line of danger."

"I understand your concern for me, Karen, but I have to go. I promised you know. If it will ease your mind, Ron Bassett is going to drive me to the hotel and pick me up again after the meeting. And now, you and I are going to have prayer and commit the whole matter to God."

They prayed, and Karen blanched as Todd took his gun from a drawer, checked it, and placed it in the holster under his coat. They hugged each other and both left the apartment.

Ron was waiting for Todd in the lobby of the White House. As they walked to the car, Todd said, "I appreciate so much your taking me to the hotel and coming after me tonight."

"I wouldn't want you to go out of the White House alone at night, especially after I warned you of danger. The talk that is around about you and your conservative influence on the President, and the hate that is associated with that talk is too real to ignore. I'll be watching this rearview mirror whenever you and I are together."

"I appreciate your warnings and your willingness to even be

with me, Ron. As far as I know, my enemies don't know of my plans for this evening. However, I am and will be alert and on my guard at all times."

They made the trip and drew up before the entrance to the hotel without incident.

"Give me a couple of hours before you come back, Ron," Todd said as he stepped out of the car. "You can meet me in the lobby."

"Take care," Ron responded as he drove off.

Todd checked his watch. It was 7:50 as he entered the hotel lobby. He was keyed up, alert, his eyes taking in everything. Not many people were in the lobby at that time. He noted that the three elevators were at the wall directly across the lobby from the front doors.

As Todd walked across, he became aware of two men coming toward the elevator from opposite sides of the lobby. In his peripheral vision he noticed that they were big men, dressed in suits, who would arrive at the elevators shortly after he did.

As Todd arrived, the middle elevator door opened and a man hurried out. Todd went in, punched the button for the twelfth floor and turned around to face the two men entering the elevator. He had no doubts about what he was facing. One man was drawing his hand out of his side pocket, and Todd saw the butt of a gun. There was no doubt that the men were together.

Todd took in the situation instantly and knew he would have only one chance and that would be just as the door closed. In movements so fast that the men had no chance to act, Todd's foot slammed into the hand of the man on his right who was drawing the gun. The man grunted with pain as the gun dropped to the floor of the elevator. In almost the same movement, Todd smashed his fist into the nose of the man on his left, forcing his head to crash against the wall.

The man who had lost his gun charged at Todd, only to be met with a kick to the midsection. Todd then grabbed his arm and twisting it, felt the arm break as he hurled him into the other man, who then hit the wall and fell unconscious to the floor.

The man on the left was groggy but was fumbling for his gun, and was still standing. Todd hit him squarely on the jaw, again banging his head against the wall. The man fell unconscious to the floor, his gun coming loose beside him.

The elevator stopped at the twelfth floor and the doors opened. Fortunately, no one was waiting there. Todd got out of the elevator, reached around and pressed the button for the first floor and removed his arm before the doors closed. He then found a rest room and went in to straighten his tie and brush off his coat before going to the meeting.

Meanwhile, the elevator with the two unconscious men went down to the first floor. Two men and their wives were waiting for the elevator. The door opened, and the women screamed. The men held the doors open and called for help. The people at the desk came running. When they saw the scene, they shouted to someone to call the police and 911.

By this time, everyone in the lobby had gathered around the elevator, wondering whether the men were dead or merely unconscious. The hotel security man arrived and warned everyone not to touch a thing.

Five minutes later the police arrived and immediately noted the guns. Shortly after, the 911 people arrived and found that the men were unconscious but severely beat up. They took both of them to the hospital.

The next morning, the papers carried a front-page story of how two men had a fight in an elevator and knocked each other out. The police were investigating.

Todd looked himself over in the mirror of the rest room and thanked God for protection. He was all keyed up and wanted to calm himself down and reconnoiter a bit before he went into the meeting.

How did these men know that he would be at this hotel on this day and at this time? Only six people knew beside himself – the two ladies and the four officers of the committee.

The ladies could be eliminated as possibilities and also Senator

Curry. It must be one of the remaining three – Cornwall, Patton, head of the FBI, or General Smith.

Todd determined to focus his eyes on these three men when he came through the door into the room where the committee was meeting.

He found Room 1201 and opened the door. The men were gathered in a circle around a huge table with the four officers facing the door as Todd came in.

Three of the officers expressed joy at seeing him. One man, the Vice-President, turned white as a sheet as the blood drained from his face and looked like he was going to choke. Todd knew that Archie was the man.

Senator Curry called to the newcomer to come around the table to where the four officers were standing. The Senator shook hands with him and then presented him to the Vice-President. Beads of sweat stood out on Cornwall's face as he struggled to regain composure and force a smile on his chubby face.

"Glad to have you on board," Archie stammered lamely. "Did you have a hard time finding us?"

"No trouble at all finding you," Todd replied as he shook hands with the Vice-President and was seated between Archie and Curry.

The meeting was just starting, and Curry introduced Todd as the President's bodyguard, and one who shared the convictions of the committee. He then introduced two other men who were there for the first time.

Todd thought, "How bizarre that I am sitting beside the man who helped set me up tonight, perhaps to be killed." He decided not to let Archie get off scot-free.

"You don't look very well tonight, sir," he addressed the Vice-President, turning and looking him straight in the face.

"I…I have had a hard day. You…uh…know that there are so many hard affairs of state to look after."

"I can believe that you have been busy. Your hand is really shaking. Can I help you in any way?"

Cornwall pulled his hand back and thrust both hands into his coat pockets. "Please, I'd rather not talk about it," he said as he fixed his eyes on Curry who was talking.

The Senator launched into an address concerning the stand and purpose of the committee. He was concerned with making sure the newcomers would know the purpose of the group and reaffirming to all the rest their stand.

"I am sure," he began, "you are all acquainted with the fact that one of our members was killed since our last meeting. I speak of Senator Custer, who was shot while driving his car. I am also sure that it was his stand with us and his conservative convictions that made him a target of a violent crime.

"The stakes are high in this struggle in which we find ourselves. I want you all to count the cost. Make sure this is where you want to be, and if it is, be very, very careful to take every precaution."

"Let me go back for a moment to review the sequence of where we are in this nation."

"One, we were a nation under God when we enjoyed much blessing. All higher and lower learning, that is, all formal education was in the hands of God-fearing and Bible-teaching people. Illiteracy was at a minimum in this nation and America was blessed as no other nation in the world was blessed."

"Two, with the rise of the public school system, things began to change. Humanists and Secularists were attracted to the teaching and political careers. Along with them came the teaching of the theory of evolution, and eventually, with the help of the Supreme Court, the crowding out of anything religious in the school, much less the mention of God or the Bible."

"Three, with the removal of God and the Bible, the inevitable result was the elimination of any moral absolutes. No longer could the boy or girl say that anything was right or wrong. Anyone who spoke of an absolute in morals was considered a bigot."

"There was the devaluation of human life, no absolutes as to the definition of what consists of a family, no right or wrong in connection with sex, no one to blame for the crime he commits, society excusing lying, cheating, stealing, killing."

"In short, this is the kind of Godless nation we have today, with the spirit of anarchy all around us."

"As a committee, we represent many people in our nation who feel helpless as the Constitution is ignored by government, and forces are at work to scrap the Constitution and take over this government in any way they can. We exist to stop any such movement or takeover if we possible can."

"Here we stand. Are there any questions?" Curry looked around the circle. No one spoke. He then called on Chuck Patton, the head of the FBI to pray. He prayed fervently for the nation and for the committee that they might have protection and guidance.

Several reports were given, some decisions made, and then they adjourned.

The Vice-President headed for the door as quickly as he could and joined his bodyguards who were waiting in the hall. He noted that the middle elevator was out of order.

Todd whispered to the Senator that he wanted to see the other three officers of the committee after the rest of the men were gone.

Todd was soon alone with the three officers, and he rehearsed his experience in the elevator and the outcome.

He then told them that as far as he knew there were only four men who knew he was coming to the meeting tonight and that after the elevator incident he determined to carefully watch the faces of the four officers when he came. He noticed that three of them greeted him joyously, but one turned white as a sheet and a scared look came over his face. When Todd got to the table, that person's face was covered with sweat and his hands were trembling. That man was the Vice-President.

"There was no doubt about it," he affirmed. "He is a Judas and a Trojan Horse in your committee."

The three men were shocked and silent for a moment. Thoughts immediately went through their minds of the seriousness of this disclosure. Archie knew all their names, all their plans, and he was in the second highest position in the United States.

Patton spoke first. "We knew that Cornwall was a four-flusher and a wimp, but we didn't suspect that he would even have the gumption to be a traitor and a spy."

"When you started to speak, Senator, I glanced over and saw Todd talking to the Vice-President. I noticed that Archie looked very agitated and had sweat running down his face. I wondered if he was sick," General Smith said.

Then Todd told them of his brief conversation with Archie.

"I am certain that Archie knows that I suspect him. That is why I made sure that he knew I noticed his agitation. His hands trembled so much that I called attention to it, and he put them in his pockets. Then he refused to talk anymore."

"The shocking part of all this is that Archie was willing to be party to at least a mugging and maybe a killing." Patton said.

"What do we do now?" inquired Curry.

Todd spoke, addressing the head of the FBI. "I don't know whether it is in your jurisdiction, but if it is, I would like to see you investigate those two men. I suspect they are hired hit men and have a record. Probably the police were called and the men are in the hospital somewhere. Someone may try to kill them to close their mouths."

"I also would urge your men to be very careful. Everyone of you is sure to be a marked man. If you would like, I have a fellow guard downstairs picking me up, and we can take each one of you home."

"Don't worry about us, Todd. Each of us has a bodyguard standing outside of that door right now waiting to escort us," Patton said.

"Well then, please keep praying. Do you realize that only one man stands between Archie becoming President of this country, and that man is the President. What a target he is in the eyes of the enemy!" Todd said.

There was a knock on the door. Curry went over and opened it. The three bodyguards and Todd's friend Ron came in.

"We sure are glad to see that all of you are all right. There's a lot of activity going on downstairs," one of the men said.

"What kind of activity?" Todd queried.

"Two armed men were found in an elevator all beat up. They said it looked like they had fought each other and somehow knocked each other out. The police and the ambulance came, and the men are in a hospital somewhere."

Todd noticed that Ron was looking at him intently as Ron said, "That elevator has been locked off by the police for further inspection. Do you think their presence in the building had anything to do with knowing about your meeting?"

Patton answered, "Well, one thing is for sure. They didn't show up at our meeting. Let's go down to the lobby."

There was still an air of excitement downstairs as the lobby was now filled with people. The news people were there and frustrated that the police were gone, and there was no one there, except the two couples who discovered the men, to give any answers.

Patton pulled Todd over to one side. "I'll put a couple of men on this case tonight and make sure no one gets to them."

Todd thanked him and returned to Ron. "Let's get out of here, Ron. We can talk when we get in the car. Make sure you watch to see that we aren't followed."

When they were settled in the car Todd said, "I can tell by the way you were looking at me that you think I'm mixed up in this somehow. You're right, I am. In all fairness, I think I should tell you, because I think I can trust you. You gave me warning to watch out. I asked you to drive me here as a precaution, so I'll tell you what happened."

Todd then narrated all the events of the elevator. "God was with me," he said. "Timing was just right. I knew I had to act just as the elevator door came shut and the gun was coming out of the pocket. I am responsible for the condition of those two men. I'm sure they were professional him men. We will learn more about them as the story unfolds.

"Please don't tell a soul about my involvement in this, Ron."

"You can depend upon me to say nothing," Ron answered. "I just wish I had been there to see you in action!"

"I can tell you, all our training came in handy in that elevator – martial arts, boxing, wrestling, you name it. I didn't even draw my gun. Never have I been so alert and keyed up and yet so calm," Todd responded.

Arriving at the White House, Todd made his way to his apartment. The experiences of the evening and the stress left him exhausted. He went to bed immediately.

Patton and the Chief of Police of Washington were good friends. Chuck called the Chief and told him he had just come from a meeting in the hotel and what he had found out from the hotel personnel about the strange scene in the elevator. He said he was interested in the incident because he was in the hotel attending a meeting of important men at the time the elevator incident occurred. They were not disturbed but perhaps there was some connection between the two incidents.

Chuck asked whether a guard had been posted in the hospital where the men had been taken.

The Chief said that he had not been notified of this incident, because probably a hundred other bizarre things take place every night in Washington. He said he would call headquarters to see what he could find and would call the FBI man back.

Patton thanked the Chief and said he would wait up for a call to his home. Thirty minutes later a call came. "Chuck, this is Chief Burns. That was a weird sight my men saw. Both of the beaten men, suspects, are in the hospital. A preliminary exam of their fingerprints indicates that these two are known hit men. They both had guns with silencers, and it appears that they had a fight with each other. Both were beat up pretty bad. A strange thing is, both guns were on the floor. Neither gun had been fired even though it must have been a terrific struggle."

"Because of our suspicions, and if they are hit men who were on some kind of mission, I have placed two of my men in the hospital on guard with order not to let anyone see these men except known, hospital personnel."

"I can't rule out that they may have been headed for your meeting room. I don't know who was at your meeting, but crazy things are taking place in this city, and there are plenty of people who would like to kill the head of the FBI and the police chief of Washington."

"I'm going to question them in the hospital tomorrow. Would you like to be with me?"

"I sure would," Chuck replied. "Make sure your men question and identify anyone who wants to see these men. Alert the hospital answering service to make a record of any call that comes inquiring about these men or their room numbers. Do me a favor. Send over a couple more of your men you can trust, if you can spare them. Place one by the information desk and another to back up the officers who are guarding the rooms. Tell them that the men are not to leave."

"I'll do it," replied the Chief. "I can see you think this may be something big. I'll see you at the hospital about 10 o'clock tomorrow morning."

With that, the men hung up and went to bed.

Chapter 9
"A Ray of Hope"

A Washington paper was dropped at Todd's door every morning. Todd shaved and took a shower, thinking about whether he would eat breakfast in his room or with the kitchen help. First, however, he retrieved his newspaper and began to scan it to see if there was any mention of the incident in the hotel the night before.

The paper was full of disturbing news. It had been another night of looting and robbing in the streets of the Capital. A car bomb had exploded in front of a government building, damaging the structure so that it would be closed until further notice.

An editorial gave the disturbing news that the European Alliance of Nations had now become leader of the world economically, and militarily and was the leading force in the United Nations. Other nations as well were banding together, such as the oriental nations, forming a strong block, and the Russian and Arab countries were building their war capabilities at an alarming rate.

Another article described the unrest in the country and groups arming themselves for the purpose of taking over various parts of the country. Hints of subversive groups in Washington were disturbing. One article discussed financial news, the bankruptcy of our government, and the inability to pay the interest on our debt. Nations were threatening the American government because of our inability to pay the debt to them, and they were refusing to accept the almost worthless paper money that was being printed.

Todd finally found what he was looking for, a small article in the second section. It was entitled "Two Men Found Unconscious." The article described what was found in the elevator of a hotel and the conclusion of the police that the men had a fight with each other. Just then the phone rang. It was the President's wife.

"Have you had breakfast yet?" she asked.

"No, I was just thinking about fixing something here or going down to the central kitchen," he answered.

"Karen and I are going to have breakfast here in the Presidential quarters, and you are invited. Jim will be in the meeting with his cabinet all morning. We need some company," she said.

"I'll be right over."

Breakfast was on the table when Todd entered, but food was secondary when he saw Karen. She met him at the door, clasped his hand and led him to the table where Ruth was already seated. Todd sat across from Karen, and their eyes met. His heart melted within him as he saw an understanding in her eyes and her smile. He knew she felt the same about him as he did about her.

Ruth was watching them both and couldn't resist a teasing remark. "Have I been missing something about you two, or is something going on that you haven't told me? You know, I am your friend." Ruth laughed as she spoke.

The couple looked at each other as if say, "Okay, you answer Ruth's question."

Finally, Karen spoke. "Yes, Ruth, something is going on. Todd and I haven't seen each other many times, but we are fond of one another and asking God to lead us concerning the future. Did I put that all right, Todd?"

"You did a beautiful job of stating how things are, Karen. However, Ruth, I must admit that when I look into Karen's eyes, time seems to stand still. Does that tell you anything about me? I think I could use some motherly advice," Todd chuckled as he looked at Ruth.

"I'm full of motherly advice," Ruth stated smiling. "I will be glad to share my wisdom with either or both of you. However, I can see you are both doing quite well on your own. I'll pray, and then we can start eating."

"How did the meeting go last night?" Ruth asked.

Todd was almost certain they would ask that question, and he debated how much he should answer. It was obvious it was much upon their minds, and he had fairly well determined that they had a right to know all that was going on. "Well, I had a very interesting evening, not only at the meeting but also before I reached the place where it was held."

"Todd, you sound so mysterious. What happened?" Karen questioned.

Todd then proceeded to narrate each detail of the event in the elevator of the hotel. Then he pulled out the clipping from the newspaper that he had read that morning. The ladies were aghast.

"They might have killed you," Karen muttered.

"Yes, they might if I had waited one second more. Ruth, that's not all," he exclaimed. "Let me tell you what happened when I entered the room where the Committee was meeting. There were only six people beside myself who knew I was going to that meeting – you two ladies and the four men who make up the central committee. Senator Curry, Chuck Patton, Bruce Smith and Vice-President Archie Cornwall. It had to be one of these four men who helped plot to either kill me or beat me up enough to put me out of commission for a long time.

"So I determined to watch the faces of these men when I came into the meeting. All four men were sitting together at a table facing the door as I came in. Three of them acted normal as they greeted me and made it clear that they were waiting for my arrival."

"One, however, was obviously surprised to see me. His face turned white, and I thought he was going to choke. He barely recovered as I came around the end of the table, and they placed me beside him. He stuttered as he said, 'Glad to see you here. Welcome on board.'"

"Which one was it?" the ladies asked with one voice.

"Archie Cornwall, our Vice-President. He is the Judas in the Committee," Todd explained as he arose and paced the floor.

"That doesn't surprise me," Ruth began, then hurried to explain. "He has been a dubious character ever since we have known him. He and my husband were in the Senate together and friends to a certain extent, but he is well known for shady deals and questionable conduct."

"His wife is the best thing about him, and I don't understand how she puts up with him. Jim did not choose him as a running mate in the election. Mike Burly forced his selection, and Jim was in no position to oppose it."

Todd stopped his pacing and sat down at the table. "The questions in my mind are, when do I tell the President what is going on? Will he believe it if I tell him? And will he like the fact that I have anything to do with the Committee?" Todd was grave as he spoke.

"I can put your mind to rest there, Todd," Ruth said. "My husband and I talk freely, and I have kept him abreast of about everything, except last night's events. Not only that, but he has been asking many questions about my faith. I think the time is ripe for you to talk with him, Todd," Ruth continued. "If he opens the door in your conversation about spiritual things, walk right in."

"We are scheduled to go to a meeting this afternoon, and then he wants to talk with me tonight. I'll keep that in mind," Todd said.

Security was tight about President Jackson that afternoon, and his personal bodyguard never left his side. The attack on Todd proved to him that the enemy would stop at nothing to remove anyone who stood in their way. They had reason now to believe that Jackson was not going to go along with all of their wishes.

The meeting today was with the state governors. They were concerned with the growing tension and violence in their states. The exposure of the President to danger could be great. The meetings centered around a luncheon in a huge arena with two thousand officials attending and with doors opening on every side of the arena.

Todd and Bassett stood on either side of the President and directly behind him when he was seated at the luncheon. Secret Service men were everywhere. Todd's eyes scanned the balcony continually, noting the security men and looking for any sign of danger. One thing troubled Todd and that was the sight of Bo as one of the security men. He was directly across the arena guarding a door. Todd kept his eyes on him as much as he could, watching for a movement or a signal of any kind.

A program followed the luncheon with several governors speaking briefly. Most of them expressed concern about unemployment, espionage, the almost worthless currency, armed mobs taking matters into their own hands, the increasing difficulty of keeping order with the number of police and National Guard members that they had. One governor spoke bitterly about the promise of the Federal government to back the banks and depositors. The banks were going under, and the government had no money to back up IRA's, government bonds, or deposits of any kind, leaving millions of citizens destitute. What was the federal government going to do to help the states? What could they tell their people who were going hungry and becoming more dangerous in their attitudes day after day?

Finally, it was time for the President to speak. He reminded them that he had just taken office. He acknowledged the fact that things were in a dangerous mess and that he and his cabinet along with Congress were doing their best to come up with solutions.

He gave them a bit of history over the last fifty years and the steady course downward. He pointed to the fact that government operated year after year with deficit spending, foolishly running the country trillions of dollars into debt, until they could not pay the interest and had to go bankrupt.

He emphasized that previous administrations had let America's power to defend herself deteriorate to the extent that we have scarcely enough military strength to defend our own shores, or keep order among our own people. With sadness in his voice, he continued. Foolish welfare programs by the federal government had enslaved millions of Americans to a life of dependency on the government, passing that dependency on from generation to generation.

Todd had been preoccupied with security and was casually listening to what Jackson was saying. However, suddenly, he could hardly believe his ears concerning what the President now said. His voice changed. There was an intensity and much feeling in his speech that charged the audience with anticipation.

"I have not been a very religious man, I must confess. I've let my wife have the religion for us both. But, as I have looked over the history of this country and discovered its Christian roots, I have come to the conclusion that America is in trouble because America has forsaken God."

"Alex DeTocqueville, the noted French philosopher of the nineteenth century, visited America in her infancy to find the secret of her greatness. As he traveled from town to town, talking with people and asking questions, he examined our government, schools, centers of business, but could not find in them the reason for our strength. Not until he visited the churches of America and witnessed the pulpits of this land 'aflame with righteousness', did he find the secret of our greatness. Returning to France, he summarized his findings: 'America is great because America is good; and if America ever ceases to be good, America will cease to be great.'"

"I agree with DeToqueville," the President declared. "That is our problem: America is no longer good. We have taken God out of our schools, become a secular nation, violated every principle of the Bible, and are reaping the result as pictured in the Bible. 'Righteousness exalteth a nation, but sin is a reproach to any people.'"

"I don't know much about God, but as I lead this nation, I expect to know much more about Him and the Bible and govern accordingly. Some of you governors may be angry over what I have just said, but I challenge you to go back to your states and lead a movement back to God and back to the Bible. We need to entreat God for His help. In a moment I am going to call on someone to pray. But before I do, if you are with me, please stand."

Almost every person in the arena leaped to his feet and began to clap until it was a thunderous roar. Here and there were a few that remained seated with sour looks on their faces, but most came to the meeting with a feeling of hopelessness. Now they saw a ray of light, something beyond themselves.

When the applause had finally died down and it was quiet, Jackson said, "I don't know how to pray, but I know one who does. My bodyguard, Todd Bradley."

The crowd was stunned. Todd whispered to Bassett, "Keep your eyes open," then stepped up to the microphone and prayed for America, for all who were in office, for the President, and the governors as they went back to their state capitals. He thanked God for the wonderful Christian heritage America enjoyed. When he said "Amen," he led them in singing, "God Bless America." Never had that arena resounded with such singing.

The people pressed forward afterward to thank the President. Todd and Ron did their best to stay by his side and protect him, watching for the slightest movement from the crowd. One man close to the President suddenly thrust his hand in his coat. Like a flash, Todd had the man's wrist and pulled his hand out. It contained a pen. He wanted the President's autograph.

Todd apologized. The man apologized for making such a foolish move and then got Jim's autograph and wanted Todd's as well.

Todd heaved a sigh of relief when they finally got the President back to the White House. His parting words to the President were, "You made a terrific speech today. I was thrilled with the response. I'll see you tonight."

Chapter 10
New Life

About three hours after Todd entered his apartment, the President called saying he was ready to meet with the bodyguard in his office. Jackson greeted the young man warmly, and they seated themselves in comfortable chairs facing each other. "How is it going with you and Karen?" the President asked with a smile.

"Just fine," Todd replied. "I dare say your wife gives you up-date reports on that?"

"Right you are. We are very pleased that you found each other, and I won't pry any farther."

"That's okay," Todd said. "I can't think of a more enjoyable subject."

"I won't challenge that," Jim replied, "but let me change the subject. What did you think of the meeting this afternoon with the governors?"

"I thought the meeting was great, although I was nervous as a cat about security. That arena is wide open to danger."

Jim smiled as he looked across at his bodyguard. "I let you do the worrying, Todd. I did appreciate the way you handled the fellow who stuck his hand in his coat to get his pen."

"I admit he gave me a scare for a moment, and I acted on impulse. When people crowd around us like that I am always concerned," Todd replied. "I appreciated so much your speech to the governors. You almost knocked them out of their chairs with what you said. You had a very positive response from them even if there were a few who didn't like what you had to say."

"Thank you, Todd. That is one speech that I gave with sincerity and conviction. I have given many others that were written by speech writers that were pure bologna. They were written to advance our political ambitions." The President paused, then continued very earnestly. "Todd, do you remember our first talk together when I told you I didn't want you to talk to me about religion?"

Todd nodded.

"Well, I have reached a place where I have questions and need answers about this whole matter of Christ and having something that you and Karen and Ruth have that I don't have. I want you to talk to me. What do people mean when they say they have to be born again?"

Todd breathed a prayer of thanks and silently asked God for wisdom in talking with Jim. "Jim," Todd began. "That statement, 'Ye must be born again,' is from the Bible in the Book of John, chapter three. 'Born again' is something that takes place automatically when we meet certain conditions that God lays down. The Bible says that all men are sinners. Romans 3:23 says, 'For all have sinned, and come short of the glory of God.' That simply means that God is holy and righteous and that all of us have sinned and are sinners and no matter how good we think we are we could never stand in the presence of God, Who is perfect righteousness. Romans 3:10 says, '...There is none righteous, no, not one.' Do you think you are righteous Jim?"

"No."

"Are you a sinner?"

"Yes."

"Do you think God would accept you in heaven right now if you died?"

"I don't know. I'm not as bad as a lot of people I know."

"If God is perfect righteousness, are you good enough to stand before Him? There will be no sin in heaven."

"I guess I'm not good enough because I know I'm a sinner."

"Jim, God said through the apostle Paul in I Timothy 1:15, '...Christ Jesus came into the world to save sinners; of whom I am chief.' Paul, the great apostle, said that he was chief of sinners and that Christ died for Paul. We are all sinners and are lost and can't possibly go to heaven unless somehow God takes away our sins. That is why Christ came. However, your first step toward God and being born again is to admit and believe that you are a sinner and lost. Do you believe that?"

"Yes," the President of the United States said.

Todd opened his Bible to the third chapter of John again. "Jesus explains in this chapter how to be born again. John 3:16 is called the Gospel in a nut shell. Listen to what God says. First, 'For God so loved the world.' That means that God loved the world of sinful humanity. That means God loved you and me, Jim, as sinners and wanted to do something for us that would make it possible for us to go to heaven."

"Second, 'That He gave His only Begotten Son (Christ).' That means He sent His Son into this world to die for us, to take our guilt and sin upon Himself. Christ provided by his death, the gift of salvation to every person who will receive it."

"Third, 'That whosoever believeth in Him'. There is just one condition for us to be saved and that is to believe. Believe that we need a Savior. Believe that Jesus is our Savior by dying for us – claiming Him by faith. 'Whosoever' takes in everyone, including you, Jim."

"Fourth, 'Should not perish, but have everlasting life.' Which means that the moment we believe, we have everlasting life, that we are saved. Which answers your question, Jim. When we receive Christ by faith, we are 'born again' or 'born from above.' We automatically have new life in Christ, and become a child of God. This is not an emotional experience. It is a result the moment we receive Christ as Savior. John 1:12 says, 'But as many as received Him (Christ), to them gave he power to become the sons of God, even to them that believe on his name.' Now let me ask you a question, Jim. If you died tonight, would you go to heaven?"

Jim hesitated and thought a moment. "I hope so."

Todd said patiently, "do you only hope so? Now let's go over this again. You answer yes or no to these questions. Do you believe you are a lost sinner?"

"Yes."

"Do you believe God loves you?"

"Yes. He says He does."

"Do you believe Christ died for your sins?"

"Yes. He said He did."

"What did He say you would have if you believed?"

"Everlasting life."

"Do you right now have everlasting life?"

"I don't know. That seems too easy. I've led a wicked life. I'm not good enough."

Todd silently prayed, "God open his eyes." Then he said, "Jim, I want you to read the verse to me out loud and put your name in it like you were the only one on earth Christ came to save."

Jim read aloud, "For God so loved Jim Jackson that He gave His only son for Jim Jackson that if Jim Jackson believed on Christ, Jim Jackson would not perish, but have everlasting life." As he read, a look of understanding began to creep across his face.

"Jim, do you have everlasting life?"

"Yes, I do."

"How do you know?"

"Because God said so in this verse, that if I believed, I would not perish but have, right now, everlasting life. I know I am a Christian, not because I am good or because of a feeling, but because Christ died for me, and I have received the gift of salvation by faith."

Todd said, "Welcome into the family of God. You have been born again. Remember John 1:12, 'But as many as received Him, to them gave he power to become the sons of God, even to them that believe on His name."

"You see, believing is the same as receiving. Someone said a great truth, 'Salvation is not something man does for God, but something God does for man.' We are helpless to save ourselves, but God provided the two things we need to get to heaven. One, He gives us forgiveness of our sins. Christ bore our sins on Calvary. Two, He gives us a perfect righteousness in Christ — the righteousness of God when we are placed into Christ at salvation. In our lives as Christians, we are imperfect and still sin, but in our position in Christ, God sees us in Christ, and we are accepted."

The two men bowed their heads and Jim thanked God for his salvation. When he said "Amen" and looked up, his face was joyous.

Just then the phone rang. It was Ruth. "Karen is here with me and it is time you men came over for refreshments."

"Be right there," Jim said and hung up.

As they went to the President's quarters, Todd said, "You tell them, Jim, what has happened to you."

"I'll do it," Jim said. When they arrived where the ladies were waiting, Jim said, "I have something to tell you. I just received Christ as my Savior."

There were tears of rejoicing as they hugged one another. After a time of talk and refreshments, Todd and Karen excused themselves and walked to Karen's apartment. They said good night to each other, and Todd made his way to his apartment.

Several days went by following the decision of the President to accept Christ as Savior. The relationship with Todd and Karen blossomed. They exercised great discretion in their actions, knowing that their testimony as Christians was of great importance in the White House.

One morning was especially stressful for Todd as a parade was held in Washington in honor of the Queen of England. The parade ended at the Washington Monument, where a great crowd gathered and both the Queen and President spoke. The crowd broke through the rope, which separated them from the President, and crowded around him and the Queen. It was a crisis time for all the security men. Todd tried to keep his body in front of the President until finally the people were forced back.

It was 3:00 in the afternoon when Todd arrived at his apartment. He was exhausted from the tension and strain of the parade. He stretched out on the davenport and soon was fast asleep. About an hour later, his sleep was interrupted by a knock on the door. Opening it, he was pleasantly surprised to see Karen.

"I knew the President was back, so I figured you must be here too," she said. Besides, my work is all caught up for the afternoon, and I wanted to see you. How about coming to my apartment for supper? I want you to see what a great cook I am. Besides, you are probably starved. Did you get a chance to each lunch?"

"Are you kidding?" he quipped. "Every second of my time was taken up watching out for President Jackson, and I haven't eaten since breakfast. I will be delighted to come to your supper. But best of all, let me feast my eyes on you."

He stood facing her, holding both her hands looking down into her eyes, overwhelmed with her beauty and grace. He longed to kiss her, but he longed to know the thoughts that were behind those eyes that were beautiful, yet innocent and trusting and inscrutable all in one. Never would he do anything to take advantage of her or make her betray her thoughts before she was sure and ready to accept him fully. As far as he was concerned, things seemed to click with him the first time he saw her. The times they had spent together since that first meeting had made him sure that she was the girl for him.

He had met many girls and dated a few several times. Some of them had been very beautiful in his eyes, but he had looked for character and depth and had never found just what he wanted. With Karen, it was different. He not only saw beauty and depth of character, but he sensed that God had arranged their paths to meet one another, and that all this was not an accident.

He knew, however, how cautious one must be with that thought. There were many young people who tried to force their will on another by claiming that God had led them together. Todd wanted none of that in their relationship. He longed for her, but it was necessary that she have the same convictions about him.

In that moment, thoughts were racing through the mind of Karen. He had been on her mind all day. She sensed the struggle that was going through his mind as he looked at her. She knew that if he kissed her, she would not be at all offended. As she looked into his eyes and saw his handsome, boyish face and yet the sincere, honest depth of character, she longed for him, and knew that she loved him, brief though the time of their acquaintance had been.

However, she knew that she wanted to leave the decision to him. She prayed that he would make the right choice, and she knew that whatever decision he made in that moment it would be right in God's timing. Suddenly, he dropped her hands and hugged her and whispered in her ear, "I love you."

She whispered back, "I love you."

He whispered, "If I kiss you, will I offend you or disappoint you?"

She whispered, "I would love it."

Supper that evening was quite an occasion. They had opened and declared their hearts, and both were rejoicing and at rest. In their sharing, they both declared their fears for the safety of the other. These were such treacherous days, and Todd had come so close to disaster. Todd knew that anyone dear to him was exposed to danger from the enemy.

"How did it go the day the President met with the governors?" Karen asked.

They seated themselves on the davenport, and Todd spoke eagerly. "Something terrific happened. There were about two thousand people in the arena. The governors and their associates, the press corps, the security men (including Bo Campbell), and the President and Vice-President." Todd then recounted the messages of the governors and their concerns and finally the President's message. He quoted it almost verbatim. Then he spoke of the great ovation and the President asking him to pray and the song they sang together."

"It was tremendous. I've never seen anything like it." He noticed a look of concern go across her face and was about to ask about it when she spoke.

"You don't know how concerned I am about your safety," she ventured. "They tried to maim or kill you the first time. You place your life before the President's every time you go out as you act as a screen for him. The hatred for him and for you has to be increasing day by day. In you I have found someone I love and want. Thoughts and imaginations race across my mind to the extent that I don't want to answer the telephone when you are away. I am afraid of disaster."

Todd took her hand drew her close. "You are forgetting something, Karen. We both love the Lord. We both know our lives are in God's hand. He placed us here for a purpose, and we must trust Him for His care."

"I must admit that I have great concern for you, too. You know there is a Trojan horse by the name of Jennie in your office that must be aware of our relationship. The enemy would be happy to get an advantage over the President or me by doing something to Ruth or you. You both must be careful and don't leave the White House by yourself. By the way, is there anything new on Jennie?"

"Yes, there is," she replied. "We know who her contact is in the FBI, and we also know she is acquainted with Bo."

"Many things are fitting together," Todd mused. Then, jumping up, "I had better get back to my apartment in case Chuck calls me. Thanks for supper. It has been great being with you."

When Todd arrived at his apartment, he noticed on his caller ID the name of Chuck Patton, the head of the FBI.

Chapter 11
Intrigue

The alarm went off early for Todd Bradley the next morning. He had called Chuck last night, and they had arranged to have breakfast together at Smitty's Restaurant. By 7:00 they were seated across from one another in a booth removed from the other patrons. Todd spoke first. "Chuck, I've been wanting to talk with you ever since the night of the Committee meeting. What can you tell me about the two men?"

"Let me bring you up to date, Todd. I think you know that I contacted Chief Burns, my friend, and he posted plenty of security in the hospital. We did everything you suggested, and it all paid off. Let me tell you about that first. One of the telephone callers was Bo Campbell wanting to know where their rooms were. He did not get that information. His name came up on Caller ID. Another fellow posed as a doctor, and our men nailed him. He had a gun, and he is in jail."

"The two men you beat up turned out to be hit men the FBI has been looking for. They both have records and are wanted for several crimes. Burns and I questioned both of them, and I think they will implicate some of the people who are under suspicion. We think someone from the Vice-President's office made a contact with the hospital. That is being pursued."

"Personally, I'm not too anxious to nail any of these people down, except the known criminals, for awhile. I would just as soon let Bo and the Vice-President think they are in the clear. They can lead us to bigger figures."

"I think you are right," Todd commented. "I want you to give me all the information you can on a lady that works for the President's wife. Her name is Jennie Aldred."

"We are watching her," Chuck said. "She is definitely mixed up in this whole deal. By the way, Todd, you must be some fighter. Those two guys you beat up were big, strong and mean. How did you do it? They have a reputation for beating men to a pulp."

"All I know," Todd said, "is that as that elevator door was closing, I saw the possibility of two guns coming out. It was mostly instinct on my part the rest of the time. I didn't wait for them to make the first move, and I took them by surprise with a combination of boxing, wrestling and karate. Plus, the Lord was with me."

"I can believe that. When the crisis comes, I want you on my side. I have a man in my department that is a Trojan Horse I'm afraid. Jennie reports activities in the White House to him. I want you to know we are on top of that," Chuck said as he sipped his coffee.

Todd hesitated for a moment thinking of something the FBI man had just said. Then he spoke. "Chuck, you said something about 'when the crisis comes.' Could you take some time with me this morning, either in your office or in the White House, to bring me up to date on conditions as you see them in Washington and in the country at large?"

"Sure, I have some time this morning. Let's go over to my office where we can have some privacy and talk freely," Chuck said as he dropped a tip on the table and headed for the checkout.

Todd followed the FBI man in his car to the building that housed Chuck's offices. Todd had been in that building many times as he went through his course of training. However, he had never been in Chuck's office. It was a spacious place and a reminder to one of the necessities of being on guard constantly against those forces that would destroy the United States.

Chuck seated himself behind the desk and Todd took a chair in front of it so that they faced one another. Chuck spoke, "What would you like to know?"

"I want to know what we are up against. What forces are at work? How much danger we really face, and what chance there is for our nation to survive?"

"That is a large order," Chuck said calmly, "but I understand where you are coming from and why you want to know, inasmuch as you are new to Washington and the working of government and the problems we are facing here at the capital as we look at the entire nation. Let me say first of all that I am a Christian like you, and I recognize that all the problems of our country come from forsaking God and the Bible. The problems are a natural result of forsaking God's wisdom, and a punishment from God that comes to any nation that is not thankful for His goodness and thinks it can get along without Him."

"Having said that, I will try to outline where we are right now. First, there is a spirit of lawlessness that is sweeping the country. There is little respect for law and order and for those who hold office of any kind. And, I have to say, government is, for the most part, to blame. For years, men have been put in office right on up to the Congress, President, and Supreme Court who have ignored the Constitution, who lied, committed adultery, took bribes, used foul language, and were anything but a good example. That was accompanied by appointing men and women to high offices and judgeships in the government who were moral scoundrels. These were held up as role models. As a result, it is impossible to hold down crime. Violence, murders, rapes, robberies, and drugs and alcohol are so wide spread that it is impossible for law enforcement to scratch the surface. All we can do is answer calls, but it is impossible for us to track down cases."

"Most of the time the police are telling decent citizens to arm themselves and defend themselves. Many criminals are being shot, and many citizens are being killed. A goodly portion of the judges are so corrupt that it is of little avail to bring cases before them. In short, it is a jungle out there. Citizens are told to stay home at night, and the streets are almost deserted except by the criminals. Owners of businesses and shopkeepers defend their own property at night. If anyone is shot or killed on their property at night, no questions are asked."

"Second, people are getting hungry. Millions are out of work. The government is going broke and banks are failing. With life's savings wiped out, and the US currency practically worthless, it has reduced millions of people to poverty. Churches and missions are doing everything they can to feed people, and all levels of government are trying to do the same, but they can't keep up."

"Hungry people become dangerous people. If they know there is food someplace, they are going after it with any means that they have. Gangs are being organized, and they roam the cities and the countryside looking for food and other goods. You don't see much of this in the media because the media wants to put their socialist spin on everything. They are blaming our capitalist past on the present calamities."

"Todd, if the truth were known, I don't have enough men to secure the safety of Congress or the Supreme Court. Unfortunately, due to a previous administration, even our armed forces are so diminished that we would be hard put to cope with a revolution from within, especially if we were attacked by another nation from without."

"Let me give you a word of caution, Todd. We will do our best to defend the White House from outside attack, but you must guard it from within. I would suggest that White House residents stop going to church. It is impossible to guard that situation anymore. Have a minister come in and hold a service for White House residents. That is much safer."

"Third, we know that there are subversive groups that are making plans to overthrow the government. You are acquainted with a group called the Committee and probably know that within the Committee is a core group that is making plans that are not known to many of the organizations the core group claims to represent. Many decent people see only a purpose to elect liberal politicians who will advance their particular agenda. On the other hand, some of the groups are ready to do almost anything to get their own way."

"The core group seeks to unite the New Agers, the radical environmentalists, feminists, homosexuals, animal rights activists, abortionists, and many others into one force. Some of these have no idea what they would be supporting. But what I want you to see is that this core group reaches all over the nation and their purpose is to make themselves the leaders of every hungry, unhappy, disgruntled, government hating person in America."

"Apart from government, the Christian is considered their greatest enemy. That means you and me and Senator Curry and Karen and Ruth, the President's wife."

"You can add to that President James Jackson. He accepted Christ as his Savior a few days ago," Todd announced.

Chuck Patton was stunned by those words and sat quiet for a moment. "Praise God. That is the best news I've had in a long time. What a target he will be if the Committee ever finds out."

"They will. You can be assured of that," Todd responded. "Well, that is enough of that for today. Thanks, Chuck. What you have told me scares me, but I am glad to get your information. I had better get back to the President."

"Todd, one other word. These people have already killed some who stood in their way. They tried to kill you. Right now I'm thinking of Karen, Ruth, and the President. They could become targets for kidnapping or killing. I would suggest something that is top secret with just a few of my most trusted men. We can implant a chip no bigger than a pin head under the skin of each one of them that would enable us with an instrument to trace their location in the event they were kidnapped. It has a range of a mile. The signal gets louder the closer you get to the chip. Are you interested? My wife has one implanted under her skin."

"I should hope to tell you I'm interested!" Todd eagerly responded. "I'll get permission from the three of them and get back to you." With that, Todd left the office and the building and made his way back to the White House. He was sure he was being followed by a light gray car that seemed to stay with him almost to the White House. He made a mental note of the color and make of the car.

Arriving at his apartment, he called the President's wife to see if he could meet with her. She then invited him to have lunch with her and the President in their quarters. She also said that she would invite Karen as well. Todd gladly accepted.

Two hours later, as he walked toward the President's residence, the young bodyguard almost had to pinch himself to believe what was happening in his life. In a matter of a few weeks he, who was nobody, was about to eat in the executive suite as if he were a member of the family. Along with that, a girl would be there, who was the girl of his dreams and seemed to be all he was looking for. Plus, she seemed to have the same feeling about him.

His reverie ended as he knocked on the door. All three welcomed him in, and Jim motioned them to the table. "This sure looks a lot better than I would have fixed for myself in my apartment," Todd said.

"Well, what you need is a wife," Jim laughed.

"I'm working on it," Todd came back.

"Let's stop the chatter and sit down," Ruth said with a knowing smile at Karen.

Jim said, "I'm not too used to it, but I'll pray and thank God for the food." Which he did and thanked God for many other things.

After they had passed the food and had begun to eat, Ruth asked "What did you want to talk about Todd?"

"Well, I had a long talk with Chuck Patton, Chief of the FBI, this morning. He filled me in on the true condition of the United States from his perspective of what the FBI has to deal with right now. It is not a pretty picture, and it is a very dangerous and threatening time for anyone in public office. I'm sure Jim knows there are forces that want to take advantage of these uneasy and troubled times to overthrow the government." Jim nodded his assent.

"Let's all face it," Todd continued. "We are all targets for the forces that are out there. Chuck recommends that we stop attending a local church. He feels like it is impossible for security to protect you in a church setting, and it puts a whole congregation at risk. His suggestion is that we have a church service or Bible class here in the White House and invite a preacher to conduct a service or class for the residents and anyone else we want to invite. I personally agree with him."

"It sounds good to me. I certainly can see Chuck's point," the President agreed.

"I'm sure Pastor Armfield would be willing to come minister to us," Ruth added. "His service Sunday morning is at 11:00, and perhaps he would be willing to come here about 9:00. That would give him plenty of time to make it to his morning service. I will be glad to contact him."

No one objected. As soon as lunch was over, she had Rev. Armfield on the phone and presented the possibility. He was thrilled with the opportunity and said he was sure his board would go along with this arrangement. He suggested they have an informal Bible class which would give people the opportunity to contribute their thoughts and also ask questions. They agreed on starting the class next Sunday.

Mrs. Jackson spent part of that afternoon calling government people and inviting them to the Sunday Bible class. All were eager to come. Workers in the White House were also invited, and many of them said they would come.

There was another protest march that afternoon outside the gates and fences of the White House. Some of the signs and placards were ugly in their message against the President. Todd went outside then through the gate and mingled with the protesters. They did not know who he was. He had a pad of paper and pen and went about like a reporter asking what their protest was about. A few said they were hungry. Todd reminded them of things the President was doing to feed the hungry. Others said they didn't know why they were there, but had been recruited to come and parade before the news media and they would be rewarded for it. Many were hired protectors, some feminists, and some part of the so-called gay crowd. Todd asked many why they were angry at the President. Their answer was that they felt he was responsible for all their troubles. When he told them that President Jackson was a new president and had been in office just a short time and could not possibly be to blame, they were surprised but said it didn't make any difference.

Here and there Todd saw real professionals making wild statements and whipping up the crowd. The media was there with cameras, taking pictures and interviewing the crowd. Todd made an effort to count the crowd and came up with about 300 people. He watched the evening news and was amazed when they estimated the crowd at 3,000 people. He also noticed how selective they were with those they interviewed. All was given to throw the President in a bad light.

Actually, the President, working with Congress, was doing all he could to feed the people of the nation and to meet their basic needs. The problem was multiplying. Millions were out of work. Others had lost their savings with the closing of banks. The distribution of food was a problem. Hoarding of food was going on, and prices were rising. The government concentrated on keeping people from starving.

Jackson and Creationists in Congress had seen the failure of the past welfare system, which spent a great deal of its funds on the bureaucracy in Washington, and fostered dependency of families on welfare which was passed down from generation to generation. The government was actually out of money, so instead of following past failures they were organizing churches and missions and other organizations to serve meals to anyone in need, and the government tried to funnel food to these feeding centers.

In addition, they encouraged farmers to plant and raise all the food they could, and encouraged families to plant gardens on their own property and on that land the farmers might make available to them. However, as the socialists saw the possibility of power slipping away from them and returned to the people, there was a steady barrage of lies in the media against government efforts, and accusations against the President that he was unfeeling, and his efforts were degrading to all humanity. People were urged to rise up and protest. Occasionally, there would be a voice or an article that praised the efforts being made. But the overwhelming impact was in the direction of distortion of the truth and stirring up the people.

Todd went back to the White House and from a window watched them sadly. Some rocks were landing on the lawn, and the police arrived. Rocks were thrown at the police car. More police arrived and arrested some protesters. Todd knew that most of the people did not really know why they were there. But he also knew that these protests would probably increase in number and intensity. A spirit of anarchy was in the air. Todd thought of the mob that was stirred up by the priests and the religious leaders against Jesus and how they cried "Crucify Him! Crucify Him!" This ended with the crucifixion. Jesus on the cross cried, "Father, forgive them for they know not what they do."

Todd thought, so often that is true. Certain leaders have plans the people know nothing about, but they deceive the people and twist the truth, stirring the people up to fever pitch until they do something that is utterly wrong. "Another group will be here tomorrow," Todd said out loud to himself. "And it may never stop."

Todd had explained to the President, Ruth and Karen about the wisdom of installing a chip in the body of each of them. That evening, Chuck Patton and his team of experts came to the White House and installed the chips.

Chapter 12
The Service

The residents of the White House looked forward to Sunday morning. The pastor and his wife arrived early. The largest room in the house was equipped with two rows of chairs with an opening for a pulpit or a chair, whichever the pastor desired. Guests from outside the White House joined the residents inside until about seventy people were seated in the circle.

The President welcomed the people and gave a word of explanation. Then he introduced Pastor Armfield. The pastor let them know that he would conduct the class informally, giving opportunity for input and questions from the people who were there.

He led them in prayer, and then announced they would be considering the subject "The Rapture of the Church." He then asked how many of them did not know what the rapture was. Several raised their hands. He answered, "The rapture refers to an event when Christ returns in the air and catches away all who have received Christ as Savior. It is also called 'the Blessed Hope of the Church.'"

A lady raised her hand. "What about the Christians who have

died?"

"They will be raised first," Armfield replied. "That is made very clear in I Thessalonians 4:16,17. Turn in your Bibles and read with me. '*For the Lord himself shall descend from heaven with a shout, with the voice of the archangel, and with the trump of God; and the dead in Christ shall rise first: Then we which are alive and remain shall be caught up together with them in the clouds, to meet the Lord in the air: and so shall we ever be with the Lord.*'

"You see this passage lays it out very clearly that Jesus is coming at some time in the air, and our dead loved ones who knew the Lord will be raised and meet Christ first. Then every living Christian will suddenly be missing. They will be 'raptured,' gone to meet Jesus in the air to go and be with Him in heaven."

"I have never heard that before," came from a lady in the second row. "Isn't that rather far fetched? Is that spoken of in other places in the Bible?"

Armfield was very pleasant and kind in his answer. "Thank you for your question. It really is two questions. One, 'Isn't that far fetched?' It may sound that way to us, but all things are possible with God. Don't you think it must have sounded far fetched in the Old Testament when God said that the Messiah would be born of a virgin? But that was exactly how Jesus was born."

"Two, 'Is that taught elsewhere in the Bible?' The answer is yes. I think it would be good for us to go to the words of Jesus in John 14:1-3." The people had brought their Bibles, and all turned to that passage.

"The background of this passage is that Jesus has told His disciples that He is going to be crucified and then will rise from the dead. He has also told them He is going away. Their hearts are sad, and now he encourages them. '*Let not your heart be troubled: ye believe in God, believe also in me. In my Father's house are many mansions: if it were not so, I would have told you. I go to prepare a place for you. And if I go and prepare a place for you, I will come again, and receive you unto myself; that where I am, there ye may be also.*'

"This was the hope that Jesus left in the minds of His disciples. He did not say when. It could have occurred during their time, but that wasn't God's plan. It could take place before this meeting is over, and if it did, every person who is a Christian would be gone. Nothing has to be fulfilled before that takes place. It is the Imminent Return of Christ for His own children. The word 'imminent' means, it could take place at any time. Nothing has to take place before it occurs."

He then took them to several other passages, explaining them and taking questions. Some that he covered were:

I Corinthians 1:7 – "*So that ye come behind in no gift, waiting for the coming of our Lord Jesus Christ.*"

I Corinthians 15:51, 52 – "*Behold, I show you a mystery; We shall not all sleep, but we shall all be changed. In a moment, in the twinkling of an eye, at the last trump: for the trumpet shall sound, and the dead shall be raised incorruptible, and we shall be changed.*"

I Corinthians 16:22 – "*If any man love not the Lord Jesus Christ, let him be Anathema (accursed) Maranatha (our Lord cometh).*"

Philippians 3:20 – "*For our conversation is in heaven; from whence also we look for the Savior, the Lord Jesus Christ.*"

Titus 2:13 – "*Looking for that blessed hope, and the glorious appearing of the great God and our Savior Jesus Christ.*" [1]

The pastor went on to explain that the rapture is called the Blessed Hope because we will see Jesus, and because those living when He comes will never die but will be immediately changed. We will miss the tribulation period which will come upon the earth for the next seven years, and our sin nature will be gone, and we will never fail God again. Armfield cited one more New Testament passage that brings out this last feature.

I John 2:28; 3:2-3 – "*And now, little children, abide in Him; that, when He shall appear, we may have confidence, and not be ashamed before Him at His coming ... Beloved, now are we the sons of God, and it doth not yet appear what we shall be: but we know that, when He shall appear, we shall be like Him; for we shall see Him as He is. And every man that hath this hope in Him purifieth himself, even as He is pure.*"

After many more questions and comments, Rev. Armfield concluded the Bible class saying, "There are three lessons for us concerning the rapture. One, the way to be ready for the rapture is to receive Christ as our Savior. Two, people are troubled by many trials and even persecution as Christians these days. God holds before Christians the constant hope that at any time we may be lifted out of this world. Three, knowing that Christ may come at any time, Christians should purify themselves, live godly lives, and seek to win others to Christ. If we believe what the Bible says about the rapture, it should have an effect on our lives."

He closed the session with prayer and hurried away with his wife to make it to his service at the church. The people lingered for some time talking about the wonderful and unpredictable nature of the rapture.

Chapter 13
Sunshine and Shadow

Several weeks went by after the beginning of the Bible class at the White House. The media learned of it and came out with critical comments. Typical headings for articles were: "The President Got Religion," "Should There Be a Church in the White House?" "President Influenced by Radicals" and "The Far Right and Holy Rollers."

The heat increased on President Jackson over his decisions on bills from Congress. He signed the bills that called for less government and taxes. He vetoed bills favoring bigger government. Bills favoring morality and Biblical standards and religious freedom he signed. Bills that went contrary to decency and morality he vetoed.

The liberal humanists were incensed, and the biased media pounded him in every way possible. More and more the attack was against Christians who believed that the Bible was the Word of God. Their animosity increased when the President, in a national speech on television declared that he had received Christ as his Savior and was now a Christian.

The distance between the President and Vice-President Archie Cornwall grew greater and greater. The Vice-President, threatened by party boss Mike Burley, began to openly oppose the President. Cornwall stopped attending the Creationist Committee meetings. The officers of the committee reasoned that Archie did not want to be questioned concerning his involvement in the attempt on Todd's life. He could not forget Todd's searching eyes as he came into the Committee room and looked at Archie. Archie knew that his look of surprise and his shortness of breath and sweating gave him away as he sat next to Todd. In spite of all this, Cornwall tried to project an attitude of friendliness to the President and publicly claimed that opposition to the President's views and actions were not a lack of loyalty to the President, but an attempt on his part to be honest to his own convictions. The President ignored him.

Jennie Aldred, who worked in the office of the President's wife, was a rather plain, unassuming, forty-eight year old woman. She had never married, but had endured three disappointing romances which had left her rather bitter and depressed but still hoping.

She was an excellent typist and secretary and had worked for several firms. All of them had given the best of recommendations, and there was no blemish in her records on her character.

Though her appearance was plain, she was nevertheless neat and proper, and somewhat attractive. She came from a rural setting but had been employed in Washington for most of her working years.

Three years before coming to work for the President's wife she had joined a singles group in Washington. That was the only social life she had. Two years ago she met a man about her age who also was part of that group, who took a great interest in her and she in him.

He had been married before but divorced fifteen years ago. His name was Kurt Brenner, and he worked for the government in the FBI. He was not an agent, but he worked as a librarian in the files department.

His great ambition once was to be an agent, and he worked

toward that end but always fell short of meeting the requirements necessary to qualify. He was frustrated and somewhat bitter with the government. None of that showed when he applied for his present job. His record was clear and clean. He longed, however, to be advanced to an important administrative position in the FBI. His secret ambition was to some day take the place of Chuck Patton, the head of the FBI.

His hobby was to study the files of certain criminals and see how they worked. He pictured himself planning criminal acts and then pictured himself as an FBI agent, solving a crime.

Kurt was a humanist and in the course of time became active in the Humanist party. It was there that he met Mike Burly who took an immediate interest in Kurt because of his position in the FBI and his frustration and ambition concerning the department. Burly played on Kurt's ambition and assured him that if the humanists got control of the government, Burly would see to it that Brenner would become the head of the FBI. Burly lied and was not serious about this promise, but it was exactly the hope that Kurt was looking for.

Kurt and Jennie's relationship had blossomed over the two-year period, and they were planning marriage. Kurt shared his ambitions with Jennie and convinced her that if she got the job in the White House, for which she had applied, she could be a great help to him and the Humanist party, just the same as his position in the FBI. It was in this way that she became an informant and spy as she was now firmly ensconced in the White House. One meeting with Burly convinced her that the Humanist cause was the answer to all of the nation's problems.

Mike Burly was becoming more and more upset over the way the President was committing himself to the Creationist movement. His frustration was increased by the pressures that were coming to him from groups to whom promises had been made that Jackson would be only a figurehead for the Humanist party. Burly was getting more desperate every day. Something had to be done. He called a meeting in his campaign headquarters office of Bo, Kurt and himself. When they had convened, he turned to Bo and said, "You are the one who said you would take care of the President's bodyguard, and it would be so smooth and easy. Those two bums you hired for $25,000 will probably sing their heads off before they are through. What do you have to say for yourself?"

Bo had never seen Burly so upset. He twisted nervously in his chair. "I can't explain it. Those guys are supposed to be the best and have a long record of success. If they had squealed on us, we would have known it by this time. Besides, I had no direct contact with them. They don't know me or my name."

"Well, that's some relief," Mike muttered. "What I called you here for tonight is to see if you have any ideas on what we can do to stop President Jackson. The guy has gone berserk. He doesn't listen when we tell him what to do. He and that bodyguard are gumming up the whole works."

"I think I have the answer, not for us to do, but to hire one of the gangs to do," said Kurt, with a tone of confidence in his voice. Bo and Mike both looked at him with surprise.

"Well, give us a hint," Mike spoke dubiously.

"I think we need to kidnap the President's wife and her secretary, then we have some leverage."

Bo was skeptical and expressed it. "How do you propose to get them out of the White House so anyone can get his hands on them?"

"I have a plan in mind which I will try to have all worked out by tomorrow night that I think will really work."

"Are you sure this plan makes sense?" Burly spoke hesitantly. "I think the idea is right if we can find a way to execute it. But it defies me to think of a way."

"Just give me until tomorrow night, and I will see if I can put it all together," Kurt affirmed.

"Okay, I have no other ideas. See you both tomorrow night."

After the meeting, Kurt drove directly to Jennie's apartment. She was still up and glad to see him.

"How about a cup of coffee?" he said as he kissed her.

"I'm so glad to see you," she said. "I'll have it for you in a jiffy."

He sat down at the kitchen table as she heated the water for the instant coffee.

"Did you tell me once that your office keeps a date book for both the President and the President's wife for their engagements?"

"Yes, we do. We have it there because people are always calling in to confirm dates," she said as she poured the hot water on their coffee in the cups. "Why do you ask?"

"I have a good reason. Do you suppose you could get me a list of both of their engagements from now until the end of this month?"

"I am sure I can. Why do you want them?"

"Trust me. It is better that you don't know why. And see if you can copy them down without anyone observing you."

"I'll be glad to sneak them to you. Anyway, most of these public engagements are given to the news media so they can let the people know where the President or his wife are speaking."

"Does she have many speaking engagements?"

"Yes, she does. Ever since she became a Christian, she likes to go to places to give her testimony. She has many invitations from Christian groups. Karen always goes with her on those occasions."

"Could you get that to me by noon tomorrow?"

"Yes, I could because our office closes at noon tomorrow, and I could meet you at some private place for lunch, like here at my apartment."

"That will be great. I think it is better that we keep up our practice of not being seen together in public until we are married."

Jennie came around the table, he stood to his feet, and they hugged and kissed each other.

"You are great," he said. "See you tomorrow," and he was gone.

Kurt went back to his apartment where he worked out his plan. It could not be completed until he received those dates. He smiled in anticipation. This was his hobby, and he loved it.

"The way I see it," he said out loud to himself, "This will be foolproof."

The next afternoon at 12:30, Jennie arrived with the dates. It had been easy. Karen was in Ruth's office, and a call came from the press wanting to know the date when the President would leave for the meeting in Rome, Italy, with the leaders in the European Block of nations. She answered that he would leave the 18th of this month and come back the 25th. She then quickly copied down the rest of the engagements.

Kurt arrived shortly after and downed the sandwich which she offered him. He hurried back to his office where he finished some of his daily work with the files, then sketched out his plan with the materials he received from Jennie.

He found that the President and his wife had engagements on the same day on two occasions.

One of them he preferred, the 15th, because the President would be coming back from Rome, and undoubtedly his bodyguard would be with him. On that same day, the President's wife had an engagement at 10 AM with a Christian women's group, just outside of Washington, D.C. at First Community Church. He would have to check the location of the church that afternoon to see if it would fit in with his plans.

As he left Jennie's apartment, he decided he would drive out to the church. He found it easily, and no one seemed to be around. It was a country church. There was the church building itself where services were held. Next to it, about thirty feet away, was a multi-purpose building, with a kitchen, two rest rooms and a large room for recreation or meetings. A sign on the front of this building advertised the ladies meeting and indicated the meeting would be held in the multi-purpose building. He noted that there were three exits, one in front and one on each side.

The nearest house or building was a quarter of a mile away. Kurt drove back to his apartment and drew up his plans. His face lit up as he enjoyed exercising his favorite past time, the planning of a crime, this time a kidnapping. It was a game to him, and sometime later he would plan an elaborate solving of this crime. Right now, the kidnapping must be fool-proof without harming the victims.

Kurt could hardly wait for the evening meeting. His plan, he reasoned, would surely impress Burly that he had the skills to advance quickly into an administrative position in the FBI once the Humanists took over the country.

Finally, the three men sat down together in Burly's office.

"What do you have for us?" Mike said somewhat caustically as he looked at Brenner. In truth, he did not expect much of value to come from Brenner. Bo looked on with a smirk on his face still smarting from the derision of Burly over Bo's failure to take the President's bodyguard out of the picture.

Kurt, however, was all confidence as he pulled out his sketches and maps and plans of how a kidnapping could be carried out.

"The first problem I faced was getting Ruth and Karen out of the White House. I got a copy of the schedules of the engagements of both the President and his wife. As I went through them, I found one date when both would be out of the White House, the 15th of this month, when the President will be returning from Rome. Undoubtedly, his bodyguard will be with him, and his wife has a speaking engagement on the 15th in a small church to a Christian women's organization, in a suburban or, you might call it, rural setting. I found that Ruth's secretary always goes with her to these meetings, and they are transported and guarded by two, and at the most three, security men."

Mike and Bo looked at one another in amazement and unbelief.

"Where did you get all this information?" Mike asked.

"I have my sources that are unknown to you," Kurt responded. "I also have had to do some research and call on years of experience working with the files of criminals. Let me go on."

Kurt then outlined the procedure of carrying out the actual kidnapping at the church, the getaway, the place to hold the women and the terms of release of them. The purpose of it all would be to get the President to resign. The threat would be that if he refused, he would never see the women again.

"Of course, we know that we would never harm or kill the women. But the President would not know that," Kurt said.

Burly stared thoughtfully and mused, "We will decide whether we harm them or not." This thought he did not disclose to Kurt.

Kurt continued, "There are two things that will be your responsibility – one, to find a safe place to keep the women; and two, arrange to locate just the right gang to do the job. You know there are many in the Washington area, and I would guess that you, Mike, with all of your experience would know how to contact the right one." The last statement oozed out of Kurt with a sly smile on his face.

"I have to hand it to you, Kurt. I think you have the solution," came from Bo as he studied the plans. "It looks like you have covered all the angles."

"I am pleased," said Burly. "I'll take it from here to find the right people and get the money we need. Keep your mouths shut, and we will get together as the need arises."

That evening a formal dinner was scheduled in the White House for the top military men in the armed forces and other generals and admirals and their wives. The purpose was for the President and his wife to become better acquainted with them and to show Jim's appreciation. Todd and Karen were invited by the President and Ruth to co-host the formal affair with them, treating them by this time like their son and daughter. All the tables seated two or four people, and the lighting was candlelight, with a stringed instrument group providing the music.

The atmosphere was like that of a quiet, romantic, first-class restaurant. The waiters wore tuxedo-like black uniforms. Their demeanor was one of dignity and respectful friendliness and efficiency. There were name places for each couple or person. Todd and Karen helped them find their places. Ruth Jackson had carefully placed each one and had designated a table for two at one side of the room, semi-hidden by potted plants but giving easy view to the small platform where the program would be and where the musicians were playing. The names there were Todd and Karen. Finally, all were seated, and Todd and Karen found their places.

General Bruce Smith and his wife Grace were seated with President and Mrs. Jackson in front of the platform. "What a lovely couple that is co-hosting this banquet with you," Grace said to Ruth.

"Yes, she is my personal secretary, and he is my husband's personal bodyguard. But it is strange to us, they are like the son and daughter which we never had. We just love them, and we think they love each other. They are largely responsible for our coming to know the Lord," Ruth responded.

"I kind of surmised that," Grace offered, "and we were thrilled to know that both of you are now in Christ. Bruce and I received Christ as Savior when we were in high school, and that has been the key factor in our married life. I wouldn't be surprised at all if things will be difficult for Christians in the days ahead. People are becoming more and more bold in their denunciation of Christians." Their conversation was interrupted by the appearance of their waiter to take their orders.

In the meantime, Todd and Karen were seated at their table almost hidden in the greenery around them. "Wasn't this thoughtful of Ruth to put us in this little hideaway where we can look straight out at their table and the platform?"

"She is thoughtful and kind to put us in such a romantic setting. She never knew what I had on my mind. Karen, I'm going to ask you a question, and I hope you won't think me too bold or presumptuous." He stopped and just looked at her, taking in her beauty.

"Go on," she said as she looked him straight in the eye, smiling as she did so.

"Go on, what?" he asked.

"You know what, you rascal. Finish your sentence before I give you a karate chop that you won't forget," she laughed.

"The question is," he said, "Will you marry me?" His voice was low and serious.

"The answer is yes, with all my heart."

"Then will you accept this from me?" and Todd reached in his pocket and pulled out a little box. He handed it to her, and she opened it and squealed. "It's beautiful." It was a beautiful diamond engagement ring. She jumped from her chair, took his head in her hands and kissed him.

Ruth was sitting where she could see their table. She quickly stood up. "Excuse me," she said. "I think our couple has just become engaged." She hurried over to Todd and Karen's table. Karen held out her hand for Ruth to see. "Oh, I'm so happy for both of you," Ruth said. "We'll have to celebrate tomorrow. I want to hear what he said when he asked you." With that she went back to her table.

After the banquet, Todd walked Karen back to her apartment where they sat together on the davenport with her cuddled up against him.

"Do you have any doubts about saying 'yes,' Karen?" he queried.

"Not even a little one, Todd. My cup of joy is running over. I think we knew it was going to happen the first time we laid eyes on one another."

"I know that was true of me, Karen. I look forward to the day when I can call you my wife. Oh, what turbulent times for a young couple to think of marriage. What a restless and violent age is this in which we find ourselves."

Karen weighed that thought a moment then said, "What you say is true, and every age has its challenges, but many great marriages have been forged in such times. Our God is sufficient for any time." Little did they know how their faith would be tested.

The telephone rang. It was Ruth. "How about breakfast at eight in our kitchen for the four of us?" she asked.

Karen checked with Todd. "All is okay with us," she said.

"I had better go home," Todd said. He kissed her, then said, "Good night."

The next morning found them seated at the breakfast table in the executive suite. Jim and Ruth congratulated the couple as they came into the room and then seated them at the table. "This is rather informal, but just call it an engagement celebration," Ruth announced.

"We also have a question to ask you," Jim said. "We are flying out of here Monday to go to Jarvis Air Base. We will be there three days to observe some tests by the Air Force. Jarvis is about forty miles from Cloverdale, which is your home town, Todd. Ruth and I were wondering whether you would like to go with us. This includes you, Karen. We thought it would be nice for Todd's family to meet you."

"That would be terrific," Todd replied.

"Oh, so nice and thoughtful of you both," Karen responded as she leaned over and gave Ruth a kiss on the cheek. "I have wanted to take a ride on the President's plane for some time, and this will be special, meeting with Todd's folks."

Ruth looked rather pensive as she spoke again. "This may seem rather strange to you, but we would be quite lonely if it were not for you two. You are our best friends, and we love to make excuses for you to sit at our table with us. We have no children and have adopted you in our minds as our children."

"All of this has been wonderful for me," Karen said. "My parents were wonderful Christians, and I was their only child. They were both killed in an auto accident the year I graduated from college. I was so lonely until I found Ruth, who has been both mother and friend to me." Tears filled the eyes of both of the ladies as Karen continued. "But sorrow has enriched my Christian life and matured me. When Ruth accepted Christ, there was an even greater bonding. Sometimes I forget that she is the First Lady of the nation."

"And now that Jim is a Christian, I hang around here most of the time." Then she looked at Todd, and her eyes again brimmed with tears. "I looked at men, who crossed my path and showed interest in me, with critical, skeptical eyes. I longed to find a man who was a Christian, honest, one I could trust, who would be God's man for me." She laid her hand on Todd's arm, looked with those beautiful, tearful eyes and said, "I have found that man.

I'm so happy."

It was a heavy moment for Todd as all eyes were on him. How could he be worthy of such innocent trust? He thought of the Book of Proverbs and the verse, "Who can find a virtuous woman? For her price is far above rubies." He remembered their conversation last night when she declared she was a virgin, and he was able to say with honesty, "I, too, am a virgin."

Finally, he spoke, and his voice was husky, as Karen continued to search his eyes with hers and the Jackson's looked on. "Karen, I'm not worthy of you. A Bible verse just flashed through my mind. 'Who can find a virtuous woman? For her price is far above rubies.' That is true of you. But I can bring to you a life, with no past moral complications and a wealth of wisdom gleaned from my Christian parents about home and marriage, and a desire to have and to do for my wife something the Bible commands in Ephesians. 'Husbands, love your wives, even as Christ also loved the church and gave himself for it.'" Todd kissed her, and that broke the spell of awe and wonder that had gripped them for a few moments.

"Well, the cabinet will be waiting for me," said the President as he rose from the table. "I wish all married people could have heard what we listened to this morning. I learned a great deal, Ruth. Plan on a better husband." With that, he was gone. The rest soon left for their various responsibilities.

Sunday was a day the Bible class attenders welcomed with great anticipation. Pastor Armfield had kindled their interest in Bible prophecy the first session with the discussion on the rapture. Several Sundays had now gone by with discussions on other subjects. However, he kept announcing that this particular Sunday they would discuss what would follow the rapture – the Tribulation.

Several of those who came the first Sunday kept bringing new people each session until now the meeting place, though still arranged in a circle, had several rows. The room was comfortably filled. After he prayed, he asked them all to turn to I Thessalonians, chapter five. He then took time to review the discussion of the rapture that centered around chapter four of Thessalonians and many other passages.

He pointed out that the next event we are to expect in God's prophetic program is the coming of Christ in the air for His Church – those who have received Christ as Savior. He emphasized that nothing had to be fulfilled before that event, and that it could occur even before the day was over. He reviewed the fact that chapter four of I Thessalonians talks about the rapture, and he read again verses sixteen and seventeen. "'*For the Lord himself shall descend from heaven with a shout, with the voice of the archangel, and with the trump of God: and the dead in Christ shall rise first. Then we which are alive and remain shall be caught up together with them in the clouds, to meet the Lord in the air: and so shall we ever be with the Lord.*'"

"That day may be coming soon. If He came during this class time, every person who is saved would disappear. If you are not saved, you would remain. How would you feel?"

"It would scare me half to death," one young man in the third row said.

"Why would it scare you?" Armfield asked.

"Well, because it would be weird in the first place. Then, I would know that I had missed something that I should have had. I would wonder what was coming next," he said.

"Chapter five begins to tell us what can be expected if one misses the rapture,"

"What does he mean by the 'times and seasons' in verse one?" another man asked.

"It means that they don't know the exact time when Jesus will come, but they do know the order – first, the rapture, and then the tribulation," the pastor answered.

"Do you think Paul had taught these Thessalonians about the rapture and the tribulation?" General Smith asked.

"That is answered in verse two," Armfield answered. "Notice he says, '*For yourselves know perfectly.*' That means Paul had taught them about prophecy. '*That the day of the Lord cometh as a thief in the night.*' The only thing that could make the Day of the Lord come so suddenly and unexpectedly would be the rapture. In other words, the rapture ushers in the Day of the Lord."

"What is the Day of the Lord?" Smith pursued.

"That is a term that describes when God takes a direct hand to deal with the sin of this world. It starts with the tribulation period and goes on through the Millennium and right on to the devastation of the earth. The first seven years of it are the tribulation period when God's wrath is poured out upon the earth. Notice verse nine, where he says, 'For God hath not appointed us to wrath.' That is the wrath of the tribulation period. Christians will be raptured before that wrath begins. 'But to obtain salvation by our Lord Jesus Christ." That is salvation from the tribulation because Christ comes for us."

"What will the tribulation period be like?" a lady asked.

"The Book of Daniel says it is a time of trouble," Pastor Peter answered. "Quoting Daniel, '*such as never was since there was a nation.*' The Antichrist will come to power to dominate the world politically and religiously. He is called the Abomination of Desolation in the Book of Daniel. He comes to power with a promise of peace, and he will hate God and all who profess to worship Him. He will hate the Jewish remnant that will turn to God in the tribulation period. He will demand that everyone have the mark of the beast, which mark is an indication that one worships the beast. A person cannot buy or sell without the mark. But in the Book of Revelation it says that anyone who receives the mark is doomed to hell.

"Jesus speaks of this period of time in Matthew 24:4-20, '*And Jesus answered and said unto them, "Take heed that no man deceive you. For many shall come in my name, saying, I am Christ; and shall deceive many ... For nation shall rise against nation, and kingdom against kingdom: and there shall be famines, and pestilences, and earthquakes, in diverse places. All these are the beginning of sorrows. Then shall they deliver you up to be af-*

flicted, and shall kill you ... When ye therefore shall see the abomination of desolation, spoken of by Daniel the prophet, stand in the holy place ... Then let them which be in Judea flee into the mountains ... For then shall be great tribulation, such as was not since the beginning of the world to this time, no, nor ever shall be.'"

There was much discussion on this passage of Scripture. Then Armfield concluded. "The tribulation period is the time of God's judgement on the world, and some of that is just letting man reap the effects of his godlessness, reaping the effects of doing what he wants. Evil men destroy themselves." Armfield paused. "We are reaping right now in this nation the bitter fruit of rejecting God and disobeying His Word. The riots, murders, homosexuality, government bankruptcy, bank failures, and broken families are the result."

"But this is just child's play compared to what it will be like when the true church is gone and the tribulation begins. I urge you, if you have not received Christ as your Savior, do so now. Tomorrow may be too late, with Christian friends gone and the tribulation period upon you. For you who are Christians, remember verse nine, '*For God hath not appointed us to wrath.*' And verse eleven of chapter four, '*Wherefore, comfort yourselves together, and edify one another, even as also you do.*'"

Chapter 14
The Trip

Early Monday morning found the President and his wife, along with Todd and Karen, being escorted by the usual security force out to the army base where the Air Force One plane was kept. Arriving there, they boarded the plane and were soon on their way to Jarvis Air Force Base.

Breakfast was served on board the plane. The President and his guests were served in a special room where all the comforts of home could be found. As they were eating, the President said, "Todd, this weekend I have to give the State of the Union speech over all the main networks. I would like to talk about the farmers and rural America as to what they are doing in this crisis time. Would I be too bold to ask if Ruth and I could come to your house on Tuesday and spend the day looking over the area, going into your town of Cloverdale to see how rural people are coping with what is going on in America?"

"My folks and I would be thrilled with that. My mother would love to have you for dinner, I am sure. What about security?"

Todd replied.

"You are my main security. The press does not know we are here. I have a make-up man who will disguise both Ruth and myself, and arrangements have been made for us to have a plain automobile to drive from the airport to your home. It would involve your coming back to the base tomorrow to pick us up. By the way, there will be a car waiting for you to use today. I have talked to security about this, and they have approved if they can have a helicopter in the air watching our movements from a distance and being ready for anything. They will pick Ruth and me up before dark with the helicopter so you won't have to come back until we leave for Washington," Jim said. The plane landed at Jarvis mid-morning, and a car was waiting for Todd and Karen to drive the forty miles to the Bradley home.

Karen was quiet once they were alone in the car. Then she spoke, "I'm nervous. I hope your family will like me, especially your mother. I know how attached mothers are to their sons."

"Like you!" he exclaimed, "They will love you. They are all excited about meeting you, and you and my mother are so much alike in temperament that I can see you bonding immediately. Dad is a warm-hearted man who is always concerned that people feel at home. Tess, Tim and Tom are a little quiet at first, but they will warm up to you in no time."

Todd spent the rest of their time pointing out familiar objects and sights as they drove through farm land interspersed by wooded areas. They drove through the outskirts of Cloverdale, where Todd pointed out the high school he attended and then out the country road to their farm. Todd turned in to the lane and up to the gate, which was closed. As the car stopped, the two German Shepherds came barking and looking fierce.

Todd got out of the car and talked to them through the fence making sure that they still knew him. They did because they immediately stopped their barking and wagged their tails. Todd opened the gate, drove the car through, went back and closed the gate, then drove toward the house with the dogs criss-crossing in front of the car all the way. He drove around to the back door.

His mother, Tess, and Tom were already outside and the children had grabbed and secured the dogs.

Karen was looking with apprehensive eyes at the dogs as Todd jumped out and came around to open the car door for her. He reassured her that the dogs were secured, then hugged his mother and introduced Karen. His mother hugged Karen and kissed her on the cheek and said, "Oh, I am so glad to meet you," with such warmth that Karen was immediately at ease. Then Todd introduced his sister and younger brother, who were warm in their greeting. Tom exclaimed, "Todd told us you were a knockout, and he was telling the truth."

They all laughed, and Karen said, "Thank you, Tom."

Tess said, "Come over and meet our two German Shepherds, Karen. Once they know you are accepted by us, you will have nothing to fear from them."

Karen was not afraid of dogs, but she knew when to be cautious. She approached them with the children, and the dogs eyed her with tails wagging. She talked softly to them, and they rubbed against her.

Mrs.Bradley led the way into the house, telling Karen to call her by her first name, Sue. She explained that Tess and Tom were home that time of the day because they were being home schooled. "Show Karen to the guest bedroom," she said to Todd as he was carrying Karen's suitcase. "We are going to have lunch in a few minutes, and she might want to freshen up a bit."

Todd led Karen up the broad stairs of the old but beautiful farm home and showed her the guest room. It was immaculate and well furnished with its own bathroom. They were alone for a moment, and Todd took her in his arms and kissed her. Then he said, "Well, what do you think?"

"I think your mother and brother and sister are just great. I feel right at home already. I'll be right down. I want to help your mother get lunch," she said. Todd left and went downstairs. A few minutes later, Karen came down and went out in the kitchen. Sue put her to work. Todd was in the living room, but he could faintly hear them talking. They talked as if they had known each other for years.

Sue came through the living room to get some item she had forgotten. She whispered to Todd as she went through, "You picked a winner, son. I just love her."

Todd's father, Bill, came from the barn through the kitchen where Sue introduced him to Karen. He stayed in the kitchen, and the three of them talked a long time while the ladies prepared the lunch. Finally, Mr. Bradley came into the living room and greeted Todd. "What a wonderful young woman she is, son. I feel very much at home with her." He spoke with enthusiasm.

The call came for lunch, and they headed for the dining room. Mr. Bradley gave thanks for the food and shortly after, Todd said, "I want to thank you for saying 'yes' to my call from the plane about the President and his wife coming here tomorrow. He asked about it while we were flying here."

"You don't know how excited and scared we are to have them come," Sue exclaimed. "We will do our best to prepare a real farm dinner at lunch time tomorrow."

"I hope they understand that we are just plain country folks. This is our wildest dream to have the President and wife of the United States in our home," Bill added.

Karen spoke, "You will be surprised. They are plain, ordinary people, new Christians, and craving fellowship. She has been like a mother to me, and they call us their closest friends."

"We must not tell anyone that they are coming," Todd warned. "The President will be wearing a faded shirt and blue jeans and a fake mustache. His wife will have an unattractive wig and dark glasses. They want to go in to Cloverdale and look around. He will be asking a lot of questions and will use this trip as part of his State of the Union address this next weekend. No photographers or news men will be along. Karen and I brought our rough clothes as well. We will introduce the Jacksons as our friends, which they are."

"Much has happened around here since you left," Bill spoke

gravely. "But I will wait until the President arrives to fill you in because I suspect he will want to know all about conditions outside Washington."

"Tell us about you and Karen," Tess said with a twinkle in her eye. "I notice something flashing on her left hand."

"Well you are observant," Todd answered. "It is an engagement ring, and Karen has consented to marry me. I am a very fortunate young man."

"Have you set a date yet?" Tess pursued the subject that was most important to her.

The mother broke in, "Tess, you shouldn't ask such a personal question."

"Oh, we don't mind," Karen said. "We haven't set a date yet, but let me say we have talked about it. Tess, you would make a beautiful bridesmaid, and I look forward to being part of this family."

"Now that we have that settled," said Todd as everyone laughed, "I would like to take Karen on a tour of our farm buildings and a hike through the fields and the woods. I'll take Bell, the hound with us. He probably needs a good walk. Dad, can I do anything for you – chores or anything?"

Sue spoke up, "Tess and Tom have school work to do this afternoon. I know they won't want to do any studying while the President and his wife are here tomorrow."

"When we get back, I'm going to help you in the kitchen to get ready for tomorrow," Karen said as they went out the door.

Todd took Karen on a tour of the barn, turned Bell loose to follow them, saw the silos and corn cribs, grain barn, cows and pigs and chickens, two riding horses, shop for working on farm machinery, tractors, and all kinds of farm machinery. The dairy herd and beef cattle were in a pasture that stretched out for some distance but was easily seen from the farm house. At night, they were herded into a huge corral and feeding place behind the barn where Bell was tied.

The couple walked through the pasture and into the open fields beyond. Karen was seeing things she had only seen in pictures before. The fields of corn and wheat, the clover and alfalfa hay fields, it was all a thing of beauty that represented hard work. They came to the woods which were rich in huge oak, maple and occasionally a hickory or walnut tree. Deer tracks were everywhere, especially around the stream that flowed through the woods and the fields.

"That is our old swimming hole," Todd said as he pointed to a place in the stream which had been dug out and enlarged. They saw several squirrels and two rabbits as they walked through about a half mile of woods. "All the woods we have walked through to here my parents own," Todd said. "From this point on it's national forest. There is no road going either way for eight miles through this forest. It is great hunting territory. My dad and I have hunted all through it."

"It is beautiful and so peaceful," Karen said as she stared up through trees at the blue sky. "How could you have left such a place for the horrors of Washington?"

"Just one way," he said. "I was looking for God's will for my life, and God opened paths and opportunities that I could not deny. And look, He led me to you – next to Christ, the joy of my life. We had better start back if you are going to help my mother get ready for tomorrow."

Karen did help Sue, both in getting supper and preparing for the President's arrival the next day. Tim was home from school when they came in from their walk. He had already been filled in by Tom and Tess about what a terrific person Karen was. He discovered they were right.

Supper was filled with chatter about Washington and about life around the Bradley household. Following the meal, they moved into the living room where they had family devotions led by the father. Tears came to Karen's eyes as she remembered similar times with her parents before they were killed. Those devotions contributed so much to her life.

They all prayed, one by one, around the circle. Karen noted how many of them prayed for safety for themselves and the others. They also prayed for America and the President and those who were in office. Then they sang some Christian songs together, and in between songs told what Christ meant to them.

Before they knew it, it was time to retire. Bill put his coat on to check out the buildings and the livestock to see if all was well. Todd and Tim went with him as they walked around the property. The German Shepherds were free to roam throughout the night. Bell was tied behind the barn keeping watch over the livestock. The corral was wired to set off an alarm if anyone touched a wire that ran around the outside of the corral. There were large flood lights hung on the side of the barn that could be turned on from the house and would light up the corral. All was in order, so the men went back to the house and turned in. Todd slept in the living room on the hide-a-bed.

The next day, Todd was up fairly early to go back to the air base. Arriving there, he found the Jackson's eating breakfast in a special dining room. They invited him to join them for breakfast, which he did. Their trip back to the farm house was uneventful. Occasionally, Todd caught a glimpse of the helicopter off to one side or through the windshield at a respectful distance. It was a comfort to know it was there, although Todd did not expect trouble.

The Jackson's commented on the beauty of the country. Todd sought to prepare them for their arrival at his home, his family, the dogs, the gate, and a general description of the farm. Soon they arrived, and the German Shepherds were there to greet them. This time, however, his brother Tim was there to open the gate and then close it again.

Again, Todd drove up to the back door so the car, when parked, would be out of sight from the road. Besides, he warned the Jackson's, he wanted to take them through the kitchen. The whole family came out to greet them with Karen leading. She wore an apron and introduced the family one by one to the Jackson's. She introduced the President and his wife as her White House parents, which pleased them.

Inside the house, they gathered in the living room where the President thanked them all and then told them the purpose of his visit. He wanted to know the condition of things in the rural areas. "Are you ready to answer questions?" he asked. They assured him they were ready. "Tim, I understand you are in high school. What is it like there?"

"To be perfectly frank, it is a place to which I dread going each day. We have some good teachers, but it is difficult for them to teach with the way the kids act in the classrooms. They risk their lives and so do decent students just coming to school. I'm almost through high school, and that fact plus athletics is the only reason I go. My parents supplement my public school classes with home schooling materials. Otherwise, I would learn little."

"Tess and Tom, I understand you are home schooled. How do you look at life?" the President asked.

Tess answered. "Tom and I like our schooling at home very much. It is a relief from what we endured riding on the school bus and attending public school. We miss association with a few of our school friends, but we don't miss being beaten up, ridiculed by teachers and students for believing in God, listening to the filthy language each day, and watching the administration and teachers ignore the cheating, lying, disrespect, and outright violence that goes on right under their noses. The only place where we can enjoy association with other kids is in church activities. Apart from that, our life is our family and the farm."

The President turned to the father. "Mr. Bradley, you are a farmer. What is a farmer's life like these days? How do you view things?"

"Well, as you came in," Bill began, "you saw a strong fence and a closed gate, two fierce dogs, and as you look out this window you see our livestock in the field where we can watch them. At night we bring them into a large corral where there is an alarm system and flood light and a big hound that howls if any strange thing comes around. If we didn't stay on guard, we would be cleaned out in one day."

"What about police protection?" Jackson queried.

"The police are my friends and are doing the best they can, but they tell me not to count on them; use whatever means I can to protect my property. They tell that to all of the farmers. Every member of our family has a rifle or two, and they know how to shoot. Fortunately, the gangs and raiders know that is true of all the farmers. They have not touched us because they know there is always someone at home. If they did raid us, I don't know whether we would shoot or not. I hope we will never have to make that decision."

"Is there much hunger in your county? Are people getting desperate for food?" Jim asked.

"I would say that about thirty percent of the people in this county are hungry. You know that with the government going bankrupt and banks closing, many elderly people have nothing, their life's savings wiped out and no social security from the government because it is broke. Plus, there are many people who are out of work and not able to feed their families properly."

"Then how are these people surviving?" the President asked in dismay.

"I'll try to answer this briefly. Our church, along with some other like minded ones, got together with the farmers' association, and we prepare one meal a day, a substantial one, in the community building. It has great kitchen facilities and a large gym where we have set up tables. All who help are volunteers. They are well organized and we serve a minimum of 2,000 people a day," Bill replied.

"Where do you get all the food?" the President's wife asked.

"The farmers are providing it. There are several hundred of us, and we systematically share milk, eggs, meat, grain – all kinds of food from the farm. We give it, we don't sell it. We also have provided plots of ground where the townspeople can plant gardens, and that is working well. This year I am trying to raise all the crops I can to help with this project."

"This is great. I want to see it in action. Is this going on anywhere else?"

"This is going on, spearheaded by Christians, all across the country. But little is known about it. Do you know what our biggest problem is?"

"No, what is it?" asked President Jackson

"The government, prodded by the media!" Bill exclaimed with much feeling. "The government hits us with all kinds of silly regulations that hinder and irritate. The media accuses us of wrong motives, interfering with government efforts (of which there are none), disobeying health regulations, and the list goes on.

"It all goes back to the same problem, and that is: they want big government and government control. Even if it is at the expense of the people who need help."

The President shook his head. "You can be sure of one thing. I'll get them off your back as soon as I get back in Washington. Can we go into town and see this food system in operation?"

"We can," Jim said, "but are you sure you want to? What about security for yourself and your wife?"

"We brought some things along that I believe will disguise our identity, and I can be in touch with the helicopter every step of the way," the President assured him.

Todd went to the phone and made a call, and said to the President, "They'll be within sight in fifteen minutes. Fix yourself up, and we'll be ready to go."

The President already wore farm clothes and added a fake mustache and dark glasses. Ruth also wore blue jeans and a faded denim shirt and a ridiculous wig and dark glasses. Todd and Karen were dressed in walking clothes. Karen looked stunning. President Jackson made the comment, "No one will look at us anyway with Karen along. All eyes will be on her, especially when they know she is Todd's girlfriend."

Only Bill went with them as they got into the car. Todd drove and his father sat in front with him. The Jackson's and Karen sat in the back seat. They all noticed the helicopter in the distance as they entered the car. The President had a microphone hidden in his clothing, and he talked briefly to the people in the helicopter as they went up the lane.

Ruth carried a small camera. The President explained "Ruth will take some pictures, but nothing that will identify you or your family, Bill. I want some pictures of your food operation. I won't even identify the town. However, I will tell what is being done in various places."

As they drove toward town, they passed a place where there were garden plots. Several people were hoeing or pushing hand cultivators. Ruth wanted the car stopped so she could take a picture. Bill stood beside her so the people would know all was well.

The car they drove was plain and unimpressive. This was by design because they didn't want to attract attention. Todd drove up the main street of the small city so that the President could see the broken windows and boarded up store fronts. Few cars were on the street. Gasoline was too difficult and expensive to get. Many people loitered by the stores and occasionally groups of young people could be seen, unkempt and looking their car over with suspicion. Ruth took several guarded pictures.

Finally, they drove up to the community building. Hundreds of people stood in front as if waiting for a signal. It was almost noon.

"Drive around back," Bill said. "There is a parking lot that is protected. This car would not be safe elsewhere. We have to protect the trucks and food as it is brought in. Group 20 is responsible for the food today."

Todd drove through a gateway into the fenced in area. Everyone in the program knew Bill Bradley so they were motioned in. Getting out of the car, they entered the building through the kitchen. About 20 men and women who were working, stopped to greet Bill and Todd warmly. Todd introduced Karen as his fiancée and Jim and Ruth as her adoptive parents. Jim had been right. All eyes were focused on Karen.

One rather outspoken man chortled, "Todd, you did right well for yourself!"

Everyone laughed as Ruth's camera clicked. The two couples walked out of the kitchen into the huge gymnasium where it seemed endless rows of tables were set up. Ten serving lines were in place to expedite feeding the people. Ruth's camera shot every part of the operation, being careful to be as inconspicuous as possible.

Karen was amazed over how many people knew Todd and his father. She was also intrigued by the variety of classes of people who were there to eat that day. She remembered that Bill had said that many who once had money were wiped out by bank failures.

The President soon signaled that he was ready to go, and they made their way to the car. They drove past their church and stopped just long enough for Ruth to take a snapshot and then back to the farm. The President had talked to the men in the helicopter, and shortly after Jim and Ruth had thanked all of the Bradley's profusely, they boarded the helicopter, which had landed on the lawn in front of the house and were on their way back to the air base.

Todd and Karen decided to take one more walk back to the woods. It was a beautiful, warm afternoon. They walked through the pasture without speaking, taking in the clear air and the beauty of the green grass, the grain fields, and the woods in the background. Todd broke the silence. "Karen, I've been thinking about a question my sister, Tess, asked about whether we have set a date for marriage. Have you thought about that at all?"

"Of course I have, Todd, from the moment we became engaged."

Todd was hesitant as he asked the next question. "I know we have known each other only a few months, but ... do you want to get married sooner or later?"

"Sooner, of course," she laughed, looking up at him.

"Well," he said, testing the mood. "Would you say that about the end of next month, say the 30th, might be the best sooner?"

"Well," she said. "If the right person asked me to marry him on the 30th of next month, I would say 'yes.' I think that would give them both time for a wedding in the White House."

He grabbed her and held her tight. "I agree on the White House," he whispered. "I would like a very small wedding. How about you?"

"By all means," she said. "Especially in these times in which we live."

"I don't think my folks could leave the farm to come," Todd said. "There would be nothing left when they returned. Besides that, I think it is safer here than in Washington. We can now tell my folks the date, and they can make up their own minds."

They went into the woods a short distance and then turned back toward the house. The rest of the afternoon was spent with Todd helping his dad with farm work and Karen helping Sue in the kitchen. Todd told Bill, and Karen told Sue about the date. Both rejoiced.

The two ladies stood facing each other in the kitchen. Sue spoke, "Karen, a mother is very attached to her sons and daughters and prays much about a mate for them. I thought much about my son being in Washington and who would look after his needs even though he is a very capable and self-reliant boy. Fears often gripped me that he would meet some light-headed, pretty girl, who would not be a Christian and might sweep him off his feet, and wreck his life. May God forgive me for not having faith."

"Karen, I have only known you two days, but you are God's answer to my prayers. I love you even as I see my boy loves you. I approve of your wedding, and I am glad it will be soon." Mother and daughter-in-law-to-be stood in the middle of the kitchen and hugged each other and cried tears of joy.

The rest of the day was spent in eating supper and then having the family gathering in the living room. It was a time of mingled joy and sorrow as they realized they would part again the next day.

The next morning, Sue insisted on serving them breakfast before they left. After more tears and farewells, they were soon on their way to Jarvis Air Base. The plane was ready when they arrived, and they were soon in the air on the way back to Washington. The President spent most of the time on the plane working on his State of the Union speech. Once in a while he would ask Todd a question about his home or the farm or the town of Cloverdale. Their trip was enjoyable in the calm and clear weather both in the air and riding from the air base to the White House.

Friday night the President had his opportunity to speak over all the major television and radio networks and before both houses of Congress. He spoke briefly and to the point. He began by telling the people what he had inherited when he came into office: big government that required huge taxes to fuel government waste which had run the debt into the trillions of dollars and ultimately into bankruptcy and bank failures, thus reducing people to poverty; massive joblessness with companies failing, much of it because of government interference; riots in the streets; gangs running wild; looting a common occurrence; and talk of overthrowing the government. He did not create these problems, he assured them. They were here when he took office.

He then spoke of the spiritual and moral breakdown of America. The departure from God, which caused the break-up of families, godless schools, and spawned leaders and so-called heroes who were terrible examples. He then told of changes that had taken place in his own life and thinking which he credited to God and which he knew could change the country.

He used as an example a rural area he had visited, the devastation of the school system, the victims of moral and spiritual decay, the poverty of people where once there had been a flourishing community. He told of thousands of hungry people and a movement started by Christians and embraced by farmers to feed the thousands at least one meal a day. He mentioned that this was a grass roots effort started, not by the government, but by Christian people who were like the founding fathers of our country. He showed pictures.

He said he asked one of the leaders in this humanitarian movement what the biggest problem was that they faced. The man replied, government interference, and the media sounding the drums for them. They are so afraid this effort will thwart their socialist agenda for government that controls the life of every citizen of the United States.

He went on to say that he was ordering that agency right now to cease their interference and would work with Congress to eliminate every agency that is needlessly interfering with school systems, businesses, environments, and any number of other things. He closed by saying that he wanted to be the President that would lead the country back to God. When he finished, most of Congress clapped and cheered for about ten minutes. The others sat glumly, hating all that he said.

The opposition party had chosen a Senator to give the rebuttal to the President's speech. They had expected a liberal speech from Jackson and had selected a Senator who was an excellent speaker, but who had quite conservative convictions. This Senator, instead of giving a rebuttal, did the opposite. He supported all that Jackson had said and promised to support him in the Senate with his proposals.

Reaction across the country was divided. Some were very favorable; they had been longing to hear a man like this defend some proper convictions. Some were passive, taking it as political propaganda; they had heard bad politicians get religious and fool the people before. Others were filled with hatred. A certain committee was filled with rage. They had put this man in, and now he threatened to wreck their plans. He had to be removed and soon.

All kinds of polls were taken and the media played up the negative ones and played down the positive. Those who were close to the President urged him to pay no attention to the polls, but simply to do what was right. Several days went by, and Congress worked on bills to carry out the President's suggestions. Some passed both houses and the President signed them into law, down sizing government.

The Committee and the media raged.

Chapter 15
"Europe"

Days went by, and two big events loomed on the horizon. The President's trip to Italy to meet with the leaders of the European block of nations which would be held the thirteenth and fourteenth, Wednesday and Thursday. They would travel there on the 12th and come back on the 15th. The other event was the wedding, planned for the thirtieth of the month. Karen and Ruth accepted most of the responsibility for making the preparations.

Two days before the European trip, Todd was in the President's office talking over security measures. "We will have plenty of security men with us on this trip, Todd, but I'm going to insist on your being at my side during all the meetings that are held. Things are in even a greater uproar in Europe than they are here. We could be very vulnerable once the plane lands," the President said.

"I'm for that," Todd responded. "I feel good about the fact that we will be staying at the American Embassy building. It will be guarded by marines as well as our security men. By the way, did you know that your wife will be speaking at a women's meeting in a church on the fifteenth, the day we will be on our way back, and Karen will be going with her?"

"Yes, I knew, and I don't feel too easy about it."

"I don't either," Todd assented. "However, I have talked with Chuck Patton in the FBI, and he assures me that he will have at least three of his best and most trusted men escort them there, stay with them through the meeting and escort them home."

"That makes me feel better," Jim said. They then turned to making plans for their trip.

Todd and Karen had dinner together in her apartment the evening before he left for Europe. They appreciated the opportunity to be alone so they could talk over their plans. Karen filled him in on the progress Ruth and she had made and some of the people they wanted to invite.

"Karen, I am concerned about you and Ruth leaving the White House on the fifteenth," Todd said.

"I am just as concerned about you and the President flying to Italy for those meetings, with all the unrest that is in that part of the world," Karen countered. "Some of the countries over there would like nothing better than to shoot down the US President's plane."

"We're both in the same boat," Todd sighed. "Will you carry your gun?"

"I always do," she said. "Sometimes in my purse and sometimes, when I wear a jacket or vest, in a shoulder holster."

"That's good," he said. "Chuck Patton has assured me that he will have at least three of his best men escorting you all the way."

"When all is said and done, we have to commit each other to the Lord and His care." They prayed together and expressed their love for each other then Todd kissed her and left for his apartment to pack for his trip. Somewhat of a dark mood had settled on both of them as they considered this parting. No doubt the times they lived in contributed much. Hatred surrounded them; upheaval was all over the world. The White House was a little oasis; step outside of it, and anything could happen.

The President and Todd left early the next morning. Todd had just enough time to kiss Karen good-bye, and he was off with the group of security cars that took the President to the plane. Todd sat in the back seat with him in the President's armored car.

"We'll have breakfast on the plane," the President promised.

Todd could not help observing how the President had grown in stature (not physically) since he had taken office. He was a handsome man, about five feet ten inches tall, graying black hair, slim but muscular build, with a kind and firm face. He was a gentleman with a poise about him and a confidence that commanded respect of men. Yet, he was a humble man, and coming to know the Lord had enhanced this feature. He did not speak carelessly, but he was mentally sharp, and had an ability to think through matters and detect the fallacy of an argument. He would be no pushover in any world council, and he would represent the United States very well.

It was also interesting that he wanted and sought advice of Todd on almost any subject, more than the advice of his so-called advisors. Todd smiled to himself as he thought how ridiculous this would seem to the politicians if they knew the full story.

The President greeted all the newsmen, the Secretary of State, his security men, secretaries, and all others. Then he retired to the privacy of his room with Todd. All were served breakfast, but the President and Todd were served in the President's room.

As they ate, the President began to speak. "Todd, you remember the Bible classes we had on the rapture of the Church and the tribulation that followed?"

"Yes," said Todd. "I remember well."

"I have a question. Is it possible that we could see, even before the rapture some things shaping up that will find fruition in the tribulation period?"

"Yes," said Todd. "It is very possible that these European countries that have united may become the revival of the Roman Empire that was predicted in the Book of Daniel. Out of this is going to be a wicked world ruler who may be alive today but will not be identified until after the rapture."

"What are some other keys?" asked Jim.

"The subject of most importance is the nation Israel," Todd said. "All prophecy in the tribulation will center around Israel. I look forward to seeing how much attention will be focused in this meeting on Israel."

"I noticed on the agenda something about a treaty with Israel that is pending. It particularly has to do with the threat of Russia and several Arab countries wanting to move against Israel and take over that strategic area."

"Whew," burst from Todd. "That blows my mind because prophecy does talk about a treaty between Israel and European countries, and about the countries of the north coming down against Israel in the tribulation period. Time could be near for the rapture if that is true."

"Jim, this is a conference to be on your guard. I'm glad I am going to witness it."

The President was very thoughtful as he asked, "Todd, does the Bible say anything about the United States?"

"I have read books written by some fine Bible teachers," Todd answered, "and none of them have been able to identify the United States in prophecy. However, the tribulation period seems to encompass the whole world as far as God's judgements and the influence of the Antichrist is concerned."

"What is your guess about our country?" Jim asked.

"My guess would be several possibilities," Todd answered. "One, the US could give allegiance to the UN and the Ten Nation Revived Roman Empire and be swallowed up in its future. Or, two, the US could be destroyed by foreign powers before the tribulation or its beginning. Or, three, the US could self-destruct and be reduced to nothing by things that are already at work, such as disease. Or, four, God could pour judgements upon it because of its sin and destroy it as He has destroyed other nations that had wonderful advantages and turned away from God."

"We had better lay this discussion aside for the present," Jim said. "I need to meet with my Secretary of State before we land."

Todd occupied himself with looking over Air Force One and greeting some of his security friends. They landed at an air force base in Italy not far from Rome. Several officials were on hand to greet the President. He and Todd were seated in the back seat of a car in the midst of a heavily armed cavalcade that took them to the American Embassy.

The American Ambassador to Italy had met the President at the air base and now escorted him into the Embassy. President Jackson had informed him in advance that he desired a suite of rooms with an extra bedroom in the suite for his personal bodyguard. He had also told him that his bodyguard would be at his side in every meeting that was held outside the Embassy building. He requested a breakfast meeting with the Ambassador and the Secretary of State the next morning in the Embassy to prepare for the meeting at 9:30 AM with the ten other heads of nations.

The next morning, Todd ate breakfast with the other security men and they discussed the dangers and made plans as to how best to secure matters in a foreign country. The head of security of Italy came into their meeting, outlined his plans, and sought to synchronize their efforts. He rehearsed some of the attempts and one recent success that had been made to assassinate officials in his country. He emphasized the fact that this particular meeting, having eleven chiefs of state present, could be a target for all kinds of groups.

Todd made it clear that President Jackson insisted that Todd be at his side every moment he was outside the Embassy, and that all of the US security force have freedom to act on behalf of the President. The Italian official was quite willing to accept that arrangement.

The first meeting of the heads of state was more of a reception than anything else. None of the representatives of the other nations had met the new US President or his cortege. The meeting place had a box of seats for each leader and his aides. The President introduced Todd, along with the Secretary of State, Ambassador, and secretaries, as his aide. The recent Presidents of the United States had been weak men. They had established a reputation among the nations of having no convictions. Their word could not be trusted. Their economic policies finally resulted in the bankruptcy of the nation, and they had weakened the military to the point where the United States was no longer looked upon as a major military power. The European Economic block had stolen the economic leadership of the world with balance of trade heavily in their favor.

As President Jackson and his aides came to this first meeting, they had the distinct impression that these ten leaders looked down upon them and cared little for the input of the United States. However, Jackson was a great surprise to them. As their discussions began, they soon discovered that he was a man of strong convictions. He was brilliant in analyzing a situation and pointing out the fallacy of arguments.

Arrogant as these other leaders were with their success as a block the President voiced something to Todd during one of the breaks. "Do you notice that they don't seem to have any leadership as a group?"

Todd answered, "I do notice. It seems like they are looking for someone to take the lead. This reminds me that the Book of Daniel predicts that out of these nations will rise the Man of Sin, who will come with a program of peace and unify and lead them. But he will be the most vicious leader this world has ever known."

"It has become very evident to me, Todd," the President said, "that these ten nations have taken over the UN, and they aim to get everything under their command. I think that is the main reason they wanted us at this meeting."

The meetings went on all day and the next. They were centered around a number of subjects such as Israel and a proposed treaty with them, the great number of wars breaking out all over the world, the friendship of Russia with the Arab states, growing power among the oriental nations, the emergence of the old city of Babylon as a commercial center and its economic threat to the European Block. None of these and other issues were settled at this conference.

President Jackson found himself standing alone on most subjects. It became increasingly apparent that the ten leaders had goals and objectives that would make the European Block the strongest power on earth militarily and economically. The only reason the US had been invited to this council was to make them party to those goals. After each session, Jim would meet with the Secretary of State and the Ambassador and go over the subjects. They were in agreement with one another that all the Block wanted from them was a rubber stamp of approval for their plans. They weren't getting it from the American delegation so they were frustrated.

When Jim and Todd were alone, the President was full of questions. "Todd, the meetings are a waste of time for our country, but I can't help thinking about the Bible and prophecy. Are we seeing anything significant in the agenda we are covering?" Jim asked.

"Well, I am pretty excited," Todd answered. "We have to be careful. There is an old saying that I believe: 'Signs are for Israel and not for the Church.' That means that Christ could have and can come for the Church any time. Nothing has to be fulfilled before then. But God gives us many signs that will be fulfilled during the tribulation period. However, it may be possible that God is setting the stage so to speak, right now for what will take place soon."

"Like what?" Jim quizzed.

"Like a peace treaty with Israel, many wars, Babylon revived, Arab countries getting together with Russia, increasing power centered in the revived Roman Empire. If the stage is being set, the rapture is near. Remember I said 'if,' because we don't know for sure when Christ will come. The stage could become 'unset.'"

That was real food for thought for the President. He wondered what his place was in God's plan at this perilous time in the world's history.

The meetings were over and they boarded the plane to leave

Rome. They were scheduled to arrive back at Washington at two o'clock in the afternoon. They were two hours away from the air base near Washington, DC where they were to land, when a telephone call came for the President. It was Chuck Patton, head of the FBI.

"Your wife, Ruth and her secretary, Karen have been kidnapped. I am still trying to get the details. It took place at the church where Ruth was speaking. It appeared to be a gang. I'll be at the air base when you land."

Todd heard the conversation. They looked at each other stunned and speechless.

Chapter 16
Clouds

Back in Washington that morning, Ruth and Karen met in the lobby of the White House, looking forward to the events of that day. It was a beautiful sunny morning, and the day when the men would come home. They would meet them at the air base. It was good to get out of the White House for a while, and Ruth loved to speak to groups. Karen liked to hear her give her testimony and always enjoyed going to meetings with the President's wife.

Three security men arrived in two cars. Ruth and Karen got in the back seat of the limousine. Two of the security men sat in front. One of them was the driver. The third security man followed in another car.

They arrived at the church about five minutes before the meeting was scheduled to begin, which was 10 o'clock. The parking lot was almost filled with cars. Security men parked the two cars in front of the recreation building, where the meeting was to be held. Two men went inside the building to check it out, which was not difficult because the building stood by itself and had a small entrance in front, a rest room on each side of the entrance way, then a kitchen. The rest of the building was the recreation hall with windows and an exit on each side. The men made contact with Mrs. Wilson, the chairwoman of the meeting, and then went out and brought in Ruth and Karen.

The meeting room was filled with rows of chairs and the ladies were milling around sipping their coffee, eating doughnuts, and talking with each other. The two security men stood inside, each by the exit on each side of the room. The third man was outside guarding the front entrance of the building.

After a short time, Mrs. Wilson went to the podium to use the microphone, asking the ladies to take their seats, which faced away from the front entrance to the building. The meeting began with a song by the group, and then Mrs. Wilson introduced Ruth Jackson and Karen Parker. Karen was seated in the front row. Ruth began her talk by telling what it was like living in the White House.

The security man in front of the building was leaning up against the limousine facing the street. It was exactly 10:20. A young man on a bicycle with a sack of shopping guide papers came down the street, swerved into the church building and threw a paper on the steps, then rode down a sidewalk until he was in front of the security man, where he stopped and reached in his bag to pull out a paper but came out with a gun.

"Don't move a muscle, or you are dead," he said. The security man knew he meant it. "Lie carefully down on the pavement on your face. Don't make a sound."

A truck drove up in front of the driveway, blocking it completely. Two men jumped out. One ran to cut the phone lines to the buildings. The other came over to help the man with the prisoner. They handcuffed the security man, gagged him, and chained him to an iron rail behind the church.

At this time two cars drove up, two men in each car. At the same time a young lady in the meeting got out of her seat and went to the rest room in front of the building. After a minute she went outdoors and told the men where the security men were, one by each door. Simultaneously, four men burst in the three doors of the meeting place. Two from the front of the building and one from each side. They all had rapid fire guns, and the security men had no opportunity to even reach for their guns.

A leader called out, "If anyone moves or screams, we start shooting." The women were quiet. The security men were disarmed. The gang members carried handcuffs and handcuffed the men to the steam pipes which ran around the room.

The gang leader commanded, "All you women lay flat on the floor face down." Chairs flew in every direction as the women hastened to obey.

Karen wondered, "What can I possibly do? If I try to draw my gun, many women could be killed." So she decided to do nothing at this point.

All the women had name cards pasted to their dresses, and the girl who had left the meeting had already told them how to identify Karen and where she was sitting. Two men grabbed Karen, and two grabbed Ruth. They rushed them out of the building. The women were warned not to move. The keys to both security cars had been removed from the pockets of the men, and the gang locked the cars so no one could get in to sound an alarm. They found Karen's gun and took it from her, handcuffed both women, and pushed them in the back seat of a car with a man beside them. The men were all masked.

The rest of the men got in the other car, and they took off. They had stolen the truck and locked the cab. It blocked the driveway so no one could get out. It was a full fifteen minutes before word was given to the police that there had been a kidnapping.

They drove the two cars that they used in the kidnapping, and which were stolen cars, to a side road where they switched to two other cars that were parked and waiting for them. They blindfolded the women and drove for twenty minutes to an old estate and mansion in the country. Woods were all around it except the front, which faced the road. The house sat about a hundred yards back from the little-used, dead end, country road. The front yard was overgrown with weeds. Some of the windows of the mansion had been boarded up. Others had been broken by vandals who occasionally made their way there.

The gang led the ladies into the house, up the stairs, and into a room where there was a pile of blankets and two chairs. Their blindfolds were removed and handcuffs taken off. Karen went into action. She doubled up the man in front of her with a kick, hit the man to the side of her at the base of his nose with her fist knocking his head into the wall. Then she felt the cold muzzle of a gun in the back of her neck. A man had come in behind her.

"One more move and you're dead," he said coldly. Karen was motionless.

"She's a demon," the man said who was hit under the nose. They left the room and locked the heavy door.

The ladies had some light through the spaces between the boards that were nailed across the windows. The glass was for the most part broken out of the window, and a knot hole in one of the boards, about the size of a tennis ball, gave them a clear view into the overgrown back yard of the mansion.

Karen sat down on the floor with her back against the wall, breathing heavily from her skirmish with the men. She surveyed the dimly lit room with her eyes as she flexed the fingers of the hand that had hit the man under the nose. "Someone planned this room ahead of time for us. Look at these boards on the windows and that heavy door."

"Karen, you amaze me," marveled the First Lady. "The way you tore into those two men. I just stood there with my mouth open. You could have whipped them if the third fellow had not come in."

"I'm glad we have a little light in here from those cracks between the boards and that knot hole," Karen remarked.

"It's hard for me to believe this is happening to us, Karen. A few hours ago we were in the White House. Now we have been abducted and imprisoned in an old house, and our lives are no doubt in danger. But for some reason we are both calm, no tears, no screaming. Women aren't supposed to respond like this. Only the Lord could give us such peace."

"That is the truth, Ruth. God is our refuge and our strength. No doubt someone is going to use us as hostages to force something with your husband. Listen, I hear cars outside." Karen jumped up and ran to the knot hole in the window. She gave a running account of what was going on. "Two cars just drove up and five men and one woman got out. They are talking with the men who brought us here. It looks like the newcomers are paying the others off because our guards are getting into their cars and leaving. The man I hit on the nose is holding a rag to his face. He looked like he was warning the newcomers as he got in the car. So, we have a whole new set of guards and they look tough, including the woman."

What the ladies did not know was that the core committee had hired a group of professional thugs to guard the prisoners. They had strict orders not to harm the ladies, but were to care for their needs. They were to guard them night and day until the demands were met. In the event of a rescue attempt, the ladies were to be killed.

There was no electricity nor running water in the building. After about thirty minutes, the ladies heard heavy footsteps coming up the stairs. Karen and Ruth stepped back from the door and stood in front of the window, covering up the knot hole. A key was inserted in the lock and the door opened. Two men and the woman stood there with faces masked and the men with drawn guns. One man spoke. "We won't hurt you if you behave yourselves and your people cooperate. This woman has brought you some food. Blankets are on the floor for you to sleep on. Stay over there on the other side of the room while this woman comes in. Just pretend this is your new White House." The man gave a hoarse laugh at this.

The woman stepped in with a little card table and placed the food on it, and then brought in other items. Karen and Ruth said nothing and showed no fear. The other man said, "You gals are pretty cool customers for the fix you are in."

Ruth couldn't keep quiet. "We are cool because our lives are in the hands of the Lord. Our trust is in God."

The man guffawed at this. "You better get to praying because right now you are in our hands, and it doesn't look good for you." With that they backed out and locked the door.

"Well, the food looks good. They got it at a fast food place, and the coffee is still a little warm," said Karen. Then she prayed, "Our Father, we know that Thou art here with us in this time of trial. Be with Todd and Jim as they travel home. Comfort them, and protect us from harm. Thank you for this food. In Jesus' name we pray. Amen."

As they ate, Karen said, "We are going to do three things. First, and most importantly, pray and trust God to deliver us. Second, have confidence in our men that they will find us, remember the chip embedded in us. Finally, we will make preparations here to defend ourselves in an emergency."

The large living room downstairs had been fixed in advance in a crude way for the guards to stay in. Drapes and blankets covered the windows so that no light would show to the outside. They used candles for light at night. An assortment of used davenports and couches had been brought in to sit and sleep on. An old table and six folding chairs served for eating and playing cards. Two men were outside on guard day and night. Sixty thousand dollars was promised this group of thugs, and they had been paid one thousand dollars a piece to bind the deal from an unknown source.

Air Force One landed at the air base. The last two hours of the flight were very difficult for Jim and Todd. They had no doubt that the kidnappers were desperate men, who would be making demands on the President. The lives of Ruth and Karen might well be at stake. In fact, they did not know for sure if they were alive.

Patton met them as they got off the plane. "Come with me," he said, "and I will bring you up to date." He took them to an office at the base and rehearsed exactly what had taken place at the church as reported to him by his men. "The whole thing was perfectly planned by an expert," he said, "and carried out by one of the DC gangs. That much we know. My men never had a chance, especially with about 200 women at risk."

He then reminded them about something. "Do you remember that little pinhead size chip we put under the skin of Ruth, Karen and yourself, President Jackson? It is our key to finding them. I had the home unit beamed in on your plane and when you got within a mile, it began to respond loud and clear from your chip."

"We have two of these homing units. Only the man who built them for me and you folks, know about them. If the news got to the kidnappers, they would force the ladies to tell where it was." Chuck continued, "I have covered the northern part of the Washington area and about 30 miles beyond in a helicopter without success."

"The Air Force is going to take me up again and another copter will take you up, Todd, with the other homing unit if you want to go, and we will search the southern section, each taking a half. If either hits pay dirt, locate the spot on the map and notify the other copter. Say 'Home base,' and we will meet back at the base. Don't hang around the spot, or they might get wise and move out on us. Just remember in your search to stay within a mile of the ground. Maybe we can spot the place before dark."

They hadn't been in the air over 20 minutes when Todd's receiver began to buzz. They continued straight ahead and the sound got louder. Then he spotted the mansion on a dead end road with woods all around it. The buzz got fainter and fainter as they moved away. Todd drew a circle on the map and called the other copter. "Home base," he said and headed for the air base.

Both copters were on the ground within fifteen minutes of Todd's call. The place in question was estimated to be about twenty miles away. Chuck had prepared a special team of four men with complete equipment to be ready in case a place was located. Two of the men were specially trained for jungle warfare and night fighting. They possessed night vision glasses that aided in seeing in the dark. Chuck called them Chip and Brad and explained their specialty to Todd. All four men were dressed in dark clothing, and they had the same for Chuck and Todd.

By this time, the President had arrived at the White House by helicopter. He wanted to be there in case the kidnappers called. Todd contacted the President before he left for the mansion to tell him of their progress. The President thanked him and said, "I just heard from the kidnappers. They called me from a pay phone. Their message was that they have the two ladies who will be safe as long as we do what they say; I must not make public any of the demands until all demands are met; I must resign as President without revealing that I am being forced to resign; I must profess ill health as my reason; and the Vice-President must be sworn in as President, then they will release the hostages. If we slip on any of these, we won't see the ladies again. They gave us 38 hours to comply."

"Stay calm and keep praying," Todd said.

It was about dark as the three vehicles left the air base. Arriving near where the dead end road started, they parked their vehicles off the road in a clump of trees and waited for complete darkness. The sky was somewhat overcast, and there was no moon visible. It was about a half mile from where they were to the house. Chuck laid out the plans he and Todd had worked out.

"First, no talking on the road in. There must be complete silence. Second, when we sense we are getting near the house, we will enter the woods. We will carefully work our way to the clearing around the house. Chip and Brad will lead us single file through the woods to the clearing. Third, Chip and I will continue through the woods around to the other side of the house. Joe and Pete will position themselves in the back of the house. Todd and Brad will place themselves on this side where they can look at the side and front of the house. Chip and I will be about the same position on the other side."

"There will undoubtedly be at least two guards outside. Our purpose is to lie quietly until we locate them. When we locate them, contact Chip or Brad. It will be their job to take them out quietly."

The men went single file down the dirt road. They were all armed with a variety of weapons. All carried a pistol. Todd and Brad crawled together to the edge of the clearing. Todd had brought his instrument and reduced the sound. As he elevated it to the second floor, the buzz increased. "The women are on the second floor," Todd whispered to Brad. They lay quietly for several minutes. A passenger plane went over on a landing pattern. Crickets and other insects could be heard. It seemed such a peaceful night. Suddenly, someone struck a match to light a cigarette about fifty yards away, directly in front of them and close to the house. Todd could not see the man; the burning end of the cigarette gave indication of what way he was looking. Brad began crawling noiselessly. Todd thought the movements were like a snake for the two seconds he saw him, and then he was gone. The weeds and grass grew tall between the woods and the house, with an occasional bush as well.

Brad crawled slowly toward the man, carefully feeling every inch of the way. A strange excitement gripped him akin to stalking game. With his night glasses he could make out the man's form, could smell the cigarette smoke, and he watched the burning end of the cigarette. Now he was within six feet of the man, with a small bush between them. Brad gathered his feet under him. The man turned slightly toward the back of the house and Brad sprang like a cat upon him, giving him a blow on the side of the neck that rendered him unconscious, dropping his gun, and falling without a sound to the ground. Brad pulled a small hypodermic needle from his pocket and shot it into the man's arm, which would keep him quiet for an hour.

Exactly the same scenario was taking place on the other side of the mansion with Chip and Chuck. They carried that guard around to where Todd and Brad were and the two guards were handcuffed together and to a tree. As far as they could determine, as all six men huddled together, there were no other guards outside. There were two entrances to the building, one in front and the other in back.

They reasoned that soon there would be a changing of the guard or someone would come out to check. Todd, Brad and Joe crawled to positions at the front of the building as close to the porch as possible and hidden behind some bushes in case a flashlight was turned on. Brad was in the middle closest to the porch, and Todd and Joe on either side of him about fifteen feet away. The weeds were tall and coverage was good. Chuck, Chip and Pete did the same in back.

Suddenly the front door opened and a man stood in the doorway listening for a period of time. A dog barked in the distance, frogs croaked in a nearby pond. The man stepped out on the porch, turned on a flashlight and beamed it to one side and the other, then turned it off and came cautiously down the steps and turned to the left. When he turned, he was less than six feet from Brad. Brad sprang on him and with the same blow knocked him out. He gave him the same treatment with the hypodermic needle then he and Joe carried him to the tree where the other two men were.

Inside the building the remaining two men and woman were playing cards and waiting for one of the men to return. After a few minutes they stopped the card game and one said, "They ought to be back by this time. I wonder if they are dumb enough to stand out there smoking? I'm going out back. If you hear anything like shooting, go up and kill the women." The woman was tough, but she looked rather aghast at him. The man pushed aside the curtain and went out the back door and stood in the dark listening. All he heard was the sound of an owl in the woods. He gave a low call as he stepped off the small porch. "Dave, Jack, where are you?" He held his gun out in front of him as he walked right past Chip. Chip leaped upon him, but the man heard a slight rustle and pulled the trigger on his gun just before Chip's blow immobilized him.

Meanwhile, upstairs Karen and Ruth had been making their own preparations. Karen rolled the blankets up in such a way on the floor so that it looked like two people sleeping on the floor directly across the room from the door by the wall. They would be immediately seen by anyone who came through the door.

Karen then broke apart one of the rickety chairs that was in the room and took the two largest pieces which made quite formidable clubs. She then told Ruth her plan. "I'm going to stand to one side of the door, and if someone comes in with a flashlight, I'm going to club him."

Ruth spoke up, "I'm not helpless. I still play softball when I get a chance, and I can handle a bat. Give me the other club, and I'll hit the second one if there are two."

So they took up their positions, one on either side of the door. After about half an hour they heard one shot in the backyard below them. Then some excited voices in the room below and the feet of two people running up the stairs. Karen and Ruth both took their positions in the total darkness. The footsteps stopped at the door. A key turned in the lock and the door swung out. A man burst through with a pistol in one hand and a flashlight in the other. His pistol fired twice into the blankets, and Karen came down with her club on his arms with a terrific blow, knocking flashlight and gun across the floor. The flashlight stayed on as it careened against the wall giving an eerie light. The man scrambled to find the gun. Karen whacked him in the back of the head with the club and the club broke. The woman came through the door, and Ruth hit her in the forehead, swinging the club like a bat. She knocked the woman cold. The man was on the floor and grabbed Karen by the leg. Karen kicked him in the face with her other foot and he let go and got up. Then ensued a battle between a 200 pound man and a 115 pound girl. The light of the flashlight was just enough for them to see each other, and he was in a rage. Karen fought for her life. He made a wild swing which caught her on the forehead and sent her reeling for a second against the wall. However, when he sought to follow that blow, she was like lightening with a series of kicks and blows to pressure points that sent him reeling.

At the sound of the shot in the backyard, Todd was up and

running. He knew what could happen. He ran up on the front porch and found the door locked. It took him a moment to kick it in, and he heard steps going up the stairs. Gaining entrance, his small flashlight showed him the stairway. He heard shots upstairs, and his heart sank. Running up the stairs, he arrived just after Karen had sent the man reeling. "It's me, Karen," he called, just as the man found the gun at his feet.

Todd was across the room in a flash, smashed his fist into the man's jaw and kicked the gun away from him. The man went down in a heap and the women were both in Todd's arms crying like babies. He held them tight as other men came and flashed their lights on the scene. The woman that Ruth had hit on the forehead was still unconscious flat on the floor. Blood was coming from a cut on her forehead. The thug that Karen had fought and Todd had struck with his fist was just regaining consciousness. Brad quickly handcuffed him, and Chuck, who had also arrived, seeing Todd with both ladies safe, exclaimed, "Praise the Lord, you're safe!"

Chip and Joe came in and announced that Pete was guarding the four prisoners outside. Chuck took a good look at the woman on the floor and her companion sitting in handcuffs. He pulled out a walkie talkie and called for an M.P. army ambulance. The man had a nasty wound on the back of his head where Karen broke her club and his hands were bruised. Possibly, he had a broken jaw where Todd had struck him.

Karen and Ruth calmed down, and their sobbing turned into expressions of relief. Todd led them both arm in arm from the room, down the steps and out of the building. They stood on the porch and could see that the clouds had passed and the moon was out in all its glory.

The ladies drank in the fresh night air and marveled at how peaceful was the night. The dog was still barking in the distance. The frogs were making music in the nearby pond, and the insects were in concert.

Chip, Joe and Pete were sent after the three army vehicles.

Chuck carried the unconscious woman down the stairs and laid her on the porch. Brad led the wounded handcuffed man down the stairs and out on the porch. When the ladies saw the condition of the captives, they asked Todd if he could find some water and towels in the house. He came back with both and they bathed the head of the woman until she regained consciousness. Then they washed the wounds of the suffering man.

They heard the sirens and saw flashing lights of the ambulance coming down the road behind the three army vehicles. The man and woman were loaded on stretchers and placed in the ambulance. A doctor and nurse and two armed M.P. went with the ambulance to the army base hospital with the admonition from Chuck Patton to keep them under guard at all times. The other four thugs, still sleeping, were loaded into one of the vehicles, and Chuck drove the third with Todd and the ladies as passengers.

Arriving back at the air base, the First Lady and Karen were profuse in their thanks to Chuck and the other men. They whispered to Chuck, "Thank you for the little pin head under the skin."

Ruth, Karen and Todd boarded a helicopter to fly back to the White House. The news of the kidnapping had hit the national and international news media by noon. All through the afternoon the media featured it and messages of encouragement and hope flooded the White House before the President arrived back from Europe.

The President was at the White House when Todd called to say the ladies had been rescued. Ruth and Karen also assured the President they were safe and unharmed. The President told his spokesman to inform the news and that he would welcome his wife home in 20 minutes at the helicopter launch pad. The whole White House staff was outside waiting when the helicopter landed. The ladies alighted and the whole world witnessed the return.

A tremendous shout of welcome swelled up from the crowd. The President and Ruth and Todd and Karen stood before the cameras and microphones as the President thanked God for His goodness and thanked Chuck Patton and the FBI for their quick and successful response.

The President thanked the millions who had prayed and those who had sent messages to the White House. He then promised more details later about the whole affair, and the four of them walked into the White House and the President's quarters.

The ladies had tried to comb their hair in the helicopter and push the wrinkles out of their clothes. They looked tired and worn from their ordeal. Ruth persuaded Karen to stay all night with them in one of the beautiful bedrooms. Both expressed their need for a shower and sleep.

Todd held Karen in his arms and kissed her as she clung to him, and they whispered a few words to each other. Todd excused himself and went to his apartment. He, too, was exhausted.

Chapter 17
"Working and Waiting"

Chuck Patton had all five of his prisoners examined by army doctors that night. None was seriously injured. The air base had a secure holding area with several cells. He placed each man in a separate cell where they could not communicate with each other and placed them all under heavy guard. The woman was taken to the county jail in the women's quarters.

The news of the freeing of the two ladies hit the news about 10 p.m., also the capturing of the five people who were at the mansion. The terms they had given for the release of the two ladies pointed strongly to some political group who wanted the President removed from office. Plus, five people in custody would possibly tell all they knew to save their own necks.

The next morning, Jim and Ruth invited Todd to have breakfast with them. Karen was already there. The ladies went over every part of their ordeal. Todd went over thc rescue step by step: finding the mansion, locating and capturing the guards, and the final experience with the woman with the guards. "I want to see her and talk to her about the Lord," Ruth said. "I think she got sucked into something that was a surprise to her."

The events of the past week gradually faded from minds, pressed by the troubles of the present and the prospects of the future. One evening, Todd and Karen discussed a passage of Scripture in Second Timothy three, "But mark this: There will be terrible times in the last days."

Karen asked, "What is meant by last days?"

Todd explained, "The last days of the Church, just before Christ comes for Christians. The passage goes on to list nineteen characteristics of these days, such as, 'People will be lovers of themselves, lovers of money, boastful, proud, abusive,' etc., creating perilous times."

"These things will be intensified. They exist now, but we don't know how bad they will get. But immorality, deceit, injustice in high places is evident, along with a complete breakdown of society." Todd spoke thoughtfully, "The Bible spoke those words 2,000 years ago and described perfectly conditions of our day."

President Jackson spent long hours in consultation with his cabinet and with Congress. The crowds protesting at the White House got larger and uglier. The number of security men grew. The FBI took Jennie Aldredge into custody, tracing the knowledge of Ruth to speak back to her. Jennie had worked as a secretary for the President's wife.

She finally broke under questioning to implicate Kurt Brenner, member of the subversive committee and an FBI man who was the master mind of the plot to kidnap the ladies. Without doubt, others would be implicated, but rebellion, subversion, gangs, plots—the whole number of people involved, the spread of the whole sickness of revolution was so rapid, together with a complete breakdown of the judicial system, that it did little good to apprehend anyone.

In the midst of this, plans went forward for the wedding of Todd and Karen on the 30th. They decided to keep it even smaller than the original plans. Todd's family could not come. It was too risky to leave the farm and too dangerous to travel. Only a few friends were to be invited: Ron and Mrs. Bassett, Senator and Mrs. Curry, General and Mrs. Smith, Chuck and Mrs. Patton, Rusty and Mrs. McGiddo, June Edison, and Jake Thurston. Pastor Armfield had consented to marry them, and he would bring his wife. President Jackson would give the bride away, and his wife, Ruth, would be the hostess of the whole affair.

After the wedding they would fly by helicopter to Camp Arthur, just outside of Washington, to spend their honeymoon. It was an armed station that had beautiful quarters where the President frequently went. It had acres of woods and trails, all enclosed by high fences and guarded by soldiers. It combined luxury accommodations with privacy and outdoor beauty.

Ron Bassett had agreed to be best man, and his wife Tracy had volunteered to help Ruth as hostess. Karen had insisted that Ruth be her matron of honor because she was her best friend. The whole wedding was to take place on the second floor of the White House in the President's residence. The night before the wedding they had a brief rehearsal with just Pastor and Mrs. Armfield and the Bassetts present. Then they participated in a beautiful rehearsal dinner. The Bassetts had been invited to spend the night in a guest room of the White House.

After dinner, Karen invited the Bassetts to come with her and Todd to see her apartment. They would be living there after the wedding. Todd had become close friends with Ron because they shared common interests. They both wrestled in college. They both lived clean lives, never used profanity, neither drank alcoholic beverages, both were brought up in religious homes, and both were church goers. This was very different from most of the security men.

Tracy, Ron's wife, was like her husband in attitude about things and lifestyle. They had been married about a year, and they were well matched. Ron and Tracy sat on the davenport, and Todd and Karen sat each in a comfortable lounge chair, facing them. "I'm glad we have this chance to get better acquainted," Karen said. "I hope, after we are married, we can do some things together."

"That would be nice," Tracy responded. "We haven't found many couples to run around with since we moved into the Washington area."

"Tell us a little about yourselves," Karen continued. "How did you meet? How long did you go together? How has married life been?"

Tracy laughed. "You answer those questions, Ron. Especially the last one."

"I'll answer the last one first," Ron said, looking down at his wife. "Our married life has been great. I wouldn't trade it. Right, Tracy?"

"Right," she answered with a loving look.

Then Ron went on. "We were brought up in the same town, went to the same school, and the same church, although we didn't go very often to the church. Both our parents were very respected people, and our families were in the social life of the church, but we did a lot of other things on Sunday such as going to our cottage."

"Tracy was a cheerleader in high school, and wrestling was my life, much like yours, Todd. We started going together our Junior year and continued until we graduated from college. Then we got married."

"What kind of church did you go to?" Todd asked.

"It was called Magnolia Garden Church because of the area where it was built, surrounded by magnolia trees. I never did figure out what denomination it was. I think several denominations of people got together and started it. It was a ritzy church with lots of rich people," Ron said.

Tracy added, "It is a beautiful church, ornate and worshipfully furnished. We always had well-educated and distinguished ministers. All had PhD's and were leaders in peace movements and environmental and social movements. They don't feel that the Bible is relevant for our day, so they draw their materials from philosophy and psychology and the political scene. You would be impressed if you heard them."

Ron broke in, "They do speak about morals, but are never fanatical or dogmatic. They teach the people to think for themselves. Both of our parents were brought up in a stricter time, and they still cling to some Bible dogmas, which they passed on to us. We have hence sought to lead clean lives because that makes sense. But we appreciate the stimulating intellect of the ministers of Magnolia."

Todd and Karen had listened quietly to all their guests had said. They both silently prayed they would say the right thing when they spoke. Todd weighed his words carefully, "Do you believe the Bible is the Word of God?"

"Well, I suppose I do," Ron said, as Tracy nodded "Yes".

"If you believe that," Todd continued, "then you and I must decide that the Word of God has the truth and not the differing words of men. Man can only reason and guess about eternal matters. The Bible speaks with authority. Do you believe you are a sinner?"

"I guess we all know we do some wrong things," Tracy answered, "But measuring our lives by all that we see around us, we do a lot of right things, too."

"The Bible says," Karen spoke up, "'For all have sinned and fall short of the glory of God.' That means we all fail to come up to God's standard of righteousness and could never be good enough in our own strength to be accepted by God."

"That's why it was necessary," Todd added, "for God to send His Son, Christ, to die for our sins."

"I'm sorry," Ron responded, "Tracy and I are convinced that God is going to judge us on our own merits. We believe Jesus came simply to challenge us to live a good life and love our neighbor."

"And I think we had better get off from this subject," Tracy said a little testily, "before we get into an argument and end up not feeling good about each other."

"We certainly would not want that to happen," Todd said. "Will you do me one favor?"

"What would you like?" Tracy asked.

"Do you have a Bible?" Todd questioned.

"We both have one," Tracy replied.

"Good. Will you promise to read the Gospel of John and look for the word 'believe'?" Todd asked.

"We won't promise, but we will try to do that," Ron said, smiling. "And don't feel bad. We appreciate your interest in us. We had better go back to our room before the Jackson's go to bed."

"See you tomorrow at breakfast," Todd said. Karen hugged Tracy. Todd and Ron shook hands, and the Bassetts left.

Todd kissed Karen and left for his apartment.

The three couples ate breakfast together at 8 o'clock in the morning. The wedding was scheduled at 10:00. Pastor and Mrs. Armfield arrived at 9:30. The guests, twelve people, arrived at 9:45. All were seated in the lounge chairs in the large living room of the Executive residence. Everyone was dressed in formal attire even though the group was small. The pastor took his place, standing and facing the guests, then Todd and Ron Basset, followed by Ruth, the matron of honor.

Finally Karen came in on the arm of the President, who went through the formality of giving her away. She wore the white, flowing wedding dress that Ruth Jackson had worn years ago. Karen was beautiful, but her beauty was enhanced as her dark hair was framed in the white lace that crowned her hair.

The pastor spoke briefly about the factors that go to make up a proper marriage and the blessings of a family when the bride and groom both know the Lord. He took them through the vows. A hush fell over the room as each recognized the solemnity of the occasion. The pastor's voice broke as he prayed a prayer of dedication and blessing upon this couple.

Tears came to most of the eyes, though they could not explain why, when the pastor prayed about the dangers of the day and the pitfalls and sorrows that could face them all. Then he praised the Lord that both Karen and Todd knew Christ as Savior and that

Christ would be with them wherever they were, no matter the situation. Armfield pronounced them husband and wife and presented Mr. and Mrs. Todd Bradley.

All the guests gathered around them congratulating them. The room was full of talking as everyone said it was a small wedding, but it was the grandest, most impressive one they had ever attended. They all sat in the living room, waiting for the call for the dinner that would be served.

"Thank you all for coming," Todd said. "You are our friends, and Karen and I appreciate you so much."

Karen spoke. "Todd and I love each other very much, and our greatest desire now is to serve the Lord together. I was sobered by the pastor's prayer and his reminder of the seriousness of the day in which we live. This is a wonderfully high moment for us, but outside of the gates of this place is a very hostile and volatile world. Oh, how we need to pray for each other and to look forward to the coming of the Lord Jesus for His children, and in the meantime be faithful to God."

This opened a discussion that went on for about an hour with everyone except Ron and Tracy sharing what Christ meant to them and facing the reality of the seriousness of the times and yet the Blessed Hope that could take place at any time.

Todd and Karen both remarked, when they were alone at Camp Arthur, that it would have seemed the strangest close to a wedding ceremony to someone looking on that they had ever seen. But to Todd and Karen, they would not have exchanged it for the fanciest wedding in history.

Dinner was announced, and they moved to the dining room where many famous people had sat in the past. After dinner, the group, along with the White House staff, went down to where the helicopter was waiting and waved good-bye to the bride and groom.

The newlyweds were at Camp Arthur for almost a week, hiking along the trails, swimming, and playing tennis. They kept up on the news every day talking with the President and Chuck Patton, watching the news on television, and reading the newspapers.

Of greatest interest to Todd was the way things seemed to be shaping up internationally. The European Block looked more and more like the revival of the Roman Empire. It became more and more interested in Israel, trying to put the fate of Israel in the hands of the European Block and talking about a treaty with Israel that would make Israel dependent on them.

Todd ventured, "I think we had better cut short our time here at Camp Arthur and get back to our work, Karen. I feel responsible for the President, and I know you feel the same about Ruth."

Karen responded, "I have been feeling the same way, but I hesitated to mention it. Let's go back today."

The President heard from his wife that Karen and Todd were back, so he called Todd. "Glad to hear you are back. Could you come in to see me? I need to talk over a few things."

"I'll be right there," Todd answered. As Todd walked into the President's office and greeted him, he was impressed that Jim looked very tired and older. He surmised that the trip to Italy, the trauma of the kidnapping, and then plunging into all the problems and responsibilities of the presidency were taking their toll on him. His assessment was correct. Jim wanted to share some burdens with his bodyguard.

"Let me bring you up to date on some things," Jim began. "Internationally it doesn't look good. The attitude of Russia and the Arabs is increasingly threatening to Israel. Natural disasters and wars and troubles are breaking out all over the world."

"Here in our country things are worsening with each day. Now we have suicide bombers by a foreign religious group who think they gain favor with their god by blowing up themselves and others. The situation with the poor is getting worse, and famine is beginning to stalk the land. Gangs are foraging for food and whatever else they see. Not only that, but we have an irresponsible media that inflames the people; and protest marches are a continual threat as they block streets, overturn vehicles and burn buildings. Some areas of the cities look like they are bombed out and war torn. Government people on all levels are targets for assassination, and it is happening."

The President paused and Todd said, "Why don't you call in all the military that is scattered abroad thanks to the previous administration? They were sent on peace missions where they are endangered and not welcome and under UN command. We need them to keep peace here in the United States."

"You are absolutely right, Todd," Jim said. "I have ordered them all home, but it is not easy to get them away from the UN who feels like they have power over them. Some units are on their way home, I'm glad to say."

"How do you assess what's going on with the government and judicial system?" Todd asked.

"Congress and I are getting along fairly well. Their committees are here daily, and we are all seeking answers. I have prayer with those committees before we start the meetings. No one objects, although one or two look kind of sour. The Supreme Court has been thoroughly discredited. All thinking people know that it is their decisions that are responsible for opening the flood gates of sin and godlessness. Plus, the previous president appointed a flock of worthless, incompetent, and convictionless judges that have made a wreck of the judicial system. I read a verse in Proverbs 25:5 that aroused my interest, '*Take away the wicked from before the King, and his throne shall be established through righteousness*.'"

Todd's heart went out to the President as he considered the load he was carrying. He thought of the frustration of coming into the highest office in the land and inheriting the bitter fruit of years of godless governing with senseless spending and taxing and debt and ignoring of basic moral principles. He thought again of Proverbs 14:34, "*Righteousness exalteth a nation: but sin is a reproach to any people*."

Todd had prayer with the President and went back to his apartment to work on some reports. Karen came in at lunch time, and they ate together. Married life for them was blessed. Their small apartment would prove to be a haven from the busy life of the White House.

"How did it feel getting back to work again?" Todd asked.

"We didn't get much work done this morning," she replied. "Ruth and I spent most of our time thanking God and going over the ordeal that we went through in that kidnapping. I still can't get over the calmness and peace God gave us."

"I wish I could have seen you two in action when that man and woman came in to kill you," Todd smiled as he spoke. "From now on I can let you do my fighting."

Karen responded firmly, "Well, believe me, I was fighting for our lives. Those bullet holes in the two blankets tell you that they meant business. I was so proud of Ruth. I hope that woman survives the blow on her forehead. Ruth hit her like she was hitting a home run! It's a good thing you arrived when you did, Todd. The man was about to pick his gun up off the floor, and I don't know whether I could have stopped him. I understand that you broke his jaw."

Todd came around the table and drew his wife to him. He hugged her and said, "I love you so much, Karen. You don't know how my heart sank when I heard those two shots up the stairs. I was in a rage as I entered the room, and I vented my rage in that blow to the thug's jaw."

"I'm so glad you are my husband, Todd, and no one could love as much as I love you. God spared us for each other," was Karen's response.

Chapter 18
Crescendo

The days and weeks that followed resembled a gathering storm. Each time Todd went out of the White House with the President, the prayers of Ruth and Karen went with them. The danger could not be ignored. There was relief and thanksgiving each time they returned. One night a bullet from a high powered rifle tore through the White House, fired from a passing car. The guards at the White House shot and killed the two men in the car before they could get out of range. The next day, the media played the incident up big, making the guards the bad people for being too trigger happy.

Two Washington churches were bombed and set on fire. When the fire department finally got the fire under control, the building had been gutted, but the walls still stood gaunt and ugly like symbols of the spiritual gutting of America. Both churches had pastors who had been faithful preachers of the gospel and had fearlessly exposed the sin of America.

The dangers and troubles of the day did not overwhelm the

newlyweds in discouragement or depression. They both set aside a time early in the morning for personal devotions in which Todd read the Bible and prayed by himself in the living room, and Karen did the same in the bedroom. This was their quiet time alone with the Lord. Then they had devotions together in the evening in which they read the Bible together and prayed together. They walked in fellowship with the Lord, and the problems of life only made their spiritual life richer and their relationship with each other was with the strongest bonds.

Early in their marriage Todd said, "Karen, our world, for the most part, is within the fence that surrounds the grounds of the White House. Let's resolve to try to witness to every person who resides inside the White House and all the guards who are on duty outside." Karen enthusiastically agreed. She made inside her priority, and Todd made outside his priority.

In the course of a few weeks, they had told almost every person the way of salvation. Some were polite, but showed no interest in receiving Christ. Others were very interested and started attending the Sunday morning Bible class. Todd's opportunities were greater because there was a constant changing of security guards, and the message spread throughout the security guard family.

One day, as Todd came out of the White House to greet the security men and to talk to men he had not seen, he ran across Ron Bassett who was on duty. They had not seen each other in several weeks.

"Good to see you, Ron," Todd said. "How is Tracy these days? We've got to get together."

"Good suggestion," responded Ron. "Tracy and I have talked about it, but we all seem to be so busy. Tracy is just fine."

"How are you doing in reading the Gospel of John?" Todd asked. Ron smiled and said, "We haven't started yet. Same thing, too busy. I appreciate your interest in us, Todd, and we admire you and Karen a great deal, but we are just not on the same wave length. Maybe some day we will rethink the matter, but right now Tracy is studying Transcendental Meditation. She wants to look at some options."

Todd looked sadly at him and said, "The truth is in the Bible, which you both said you believe is the Word of God. Don't wait too long. Jesus may come today. Please trust Christ as your Savior."

"Thanks for trying, Todd," Ron said, smiling broadly. "Don't worry about us, we're okay," and he turned away. Todd went back into the house.

While they had been talking, a crowd of about 5,000 protest marchers came up to the gates of the White House fence. About 40 guards were on duty around the house, and they closed and locked the gates as the crowd approached. The crowd encircled the White House grounds and crowded up to the iron fence attempting to shake it. They shouted curses at the guards and the President. Their mood was ugly in contrast to the day. The sun was shining brightly, flowers in bloom, and the birds were singing.

Some people were attempting to scale the fence. Others were attempting by sheer numbers to rock the fence back and forth. The guards had their guns ready. They had orders to shoot anyone who came over or through the fence. They envisioned a blood bath if there was a break through. Suddenly, there was a hush that settled over creation. The birds stopped singing. About 20 of the guards disappeared, their guns dropping to the ground where the guards had stood. Here and there in the crowd a person disappeared. The leaves of the trees were motionless. A tour bus going by in the street suddenly left the street and crashed into the White House fence, crushing several people who were standing there. A police car, answering a call to go to the White House and speeding down the street, suddenly veered toward the fence, minus a driver and sped alongside the fence, killing or wounding at least 50 people.

A light plane, flying some distance from the White House, suddenly turned straight down and crashed and exploded. The crowd heard the sound and saw the smoke. The people, standing by the fence and seeing the guards disappear, were gripped with terror. They turned and fled, knocking down those who stood behind them. There was a scramble to get away.

The remaining guards were transfixed where they stood. They stared in disbelief at where their buddies had stood and the rifles on the ground. They looked at the dead and dying in front of the fence. Ron Bassett knew what had occurred. "It's the rapture," he wailed. He turned and raced for the White House. He stopped to call 911 for help for the people at the fence. It was flooded with calls. He then ran through the White House. A few bewildered people stood around. He ran up the stairs to the Executive Suite. He knocked on the door, but there was no response. He tried the knob, and the door was unlocked. There was an eerie atmosphere as he went from room to room calling. There was no answer. Terror began to grip him as he ran from that floor down to Todd and Karen's apartment. By that time, he was sobbing as he opened the unlocked door and called their name, no response. Two cups of coffee were on the table in the kitchen, half empty. The remaining portion was still warm. He picked up the phone and called his home.

Tracy answered, her voice distraught. "Ron, I've had the radio and television on. People are missing, disappearing right before people's eyes. Accidents are taking place all over the country. What's happening? You are sobbing. Could this —" her voice faltered. "Could this be what Todd and Karen talked about?"

"I'm afraid it is," he said brokenly. "I saw the President in the White House about an hour ago, and he didn't come out. I talked to Todd outside the White House and watched him go in. I am in the White House now in Todd and Karen's apartment. Neither couple is here, and half of our security guard disappeared before our eyes. Those men were Christians. I'll try to come home right away. Hang on."

Feeling weak, Ron closed the apartment door and sat down to collect his thoughts. Before him was a picture of Todd and Karen taken on their wedding day. What a beautiful couple, now in heaven. Just then he spotted Todd's and Karen's Bibles on the table. He remembered seeing all the notes and verses underlined in Todd's Bible.

"I'm going to take those Bibles," he muttered to himself. "Maybe I can find out what takes place next." His eyes fell on the small book case, and he went over and looked at the titles. He took three of them, *The Rapture and the Tribulation, Bible Prophecy Made Plain,* and *The Mark of the Beast.* "I'll take these with me also," he said to himself. "I'm sure Todd and Karen would want me to have them. They belong to no one now."

Picking them up, he hurried out of the White House. As he went past the lobby, he heard someone talking to the Vice President telling him what had taken place in the White House. Ron wasn't at all surprised that the Vice President was still around. As Ron drove toward home, he listened to the car radio. A reporter was telling of incidents in Washington. He said, "The surgeons were operating on a man with heart trouble. They had just opened his chest when the man disappeared from the operating table. He was a Christian, and he had talked to the doctors and nurses about Christ just before the anesthetic took over. One nurse was missing from the operating room and, like the thief on the cross, had received Christ as her Savior.

"Then there was the funeral that was in progress. The deceased was an elderly lady. The casket was open and the minister was preaching. The casket was just in front of the pulpit. The preacher was a liberal who did not believe in the hereafter nor the Word of God. He had preached recently about those fanatics who scared people by preaching nonsense about Christ coming in the air, and all Christians would be gone.

"The lady who died was a Christian with one son who had claimed to be an agnostic. He had made the funeral arrangements and made sure that the preacher he selected would not be a Bible-believing preacher. Many of the people who attended were Christian friends of the deceased.

"Suddenly the preacher's eyes bugged out, and he began to

shake and his words became unintelligible. He was white as a sheet. He had looked to make reference to the lady and pointed to the casket, and she was not there. A goodly portion of the congregation had disappeared also. People looked at the casket then at the chairs with people missing, and terror gripped them. Some dropped to their knees. Others ran out screaming. The liberal preacher had a stroke and fell into the empty casket." The reporter was very specific. He reported just as it was given to him.

Radio and television personnel were missing. Children disappeared from the classroom. Teachers were suddenly gone. Passenger planes lost their pilots and crashed in places all over the world. Several members of both houses of Congress were missing. Key people in the computer industry, city water and electric and gas systems were gone, and the systems began to break down without people with the knowledge to fix them. Disaster loomed everywhere.

Ron Bassett had to change routes many times before he reached home. He finally arrived and dashed into the house. Tracy was pacing up and down the house, alternating between sobbing and crying out. When Ron came in the door, she ran to him and threw herself into his arms. "Oh, Ron, it's my fault. We were fools not to believe. It's too late. What will we do?" she sobbed.

"I don't know, Tracy," he soothed as he stroked her hair. "But I picked up Todd and Karen's Bibles and three of their books. We will read them to see if there is any hope for us. I know by what Todd told me that beginning now will be seven years of terrible tribulation. It will be the worst in all the history of the world. We must study the Bible to see if there is anything we can do."

And what takes place next, as Paul Harvey used to say, "Is the rest of the story", which we will tell shortly.